BIGGLES SORTS IT OUT

Why should Lady Caroline Langdon help a thief to rob her father of jewels which would one day be hers by inheritance? From the start, Biggles was convinced that someone was not telling him the truth, and this tangled skein of human relationships was only finally unravelled after he and Bertie had flown to Africa and located a ruined German fort in the heart of the Kalahari Desert.

D1637624

CAPTAIN W. E. JOHNS

BIGGLES SORTS IT OUT

 KNIGHT BOOKS

the paperback division of Brockhampton Press

ISBN 0 340 10432 5

This edition first published 1970 by Knight Books,
the paperback division of Brockhampton Press Ltd, Leicester

Printed and bound in Great Britain by
Cox & Wyman Ltd, London,
Reading and Fakenham

First published 1967 by Brockhampton Press Ltd

Text copyright © by W. E. Johns (Publications) Ltd 1967

This book is sold subject to the condition that it shall not
by way of trade or otherwise be lent re-sold hired out or
otherwise circulated without the publisher's prior consent
in any form of binding or cover other than that in which this
is published and without a similar condition including this
condition being imposed on the subsequent purchaser

CONTENTS

THE KALAHARI DESERT

SOUTH-WEST AFRICA, of which Windhoek is the chief town, was, until the First World War when British troops took over, a German colony. To the north it is bounded by Portuguese Angola; to the south by the Republic of South Africa who now administers the territory, and to the east by Bechuanaland* which contains most of the great Kalahari Desert, hundreds of miles of brown, arid, blistering earth, a country that has dried up.

The Kalahari is not a desert in the sense of the Sahara, just rolling dunes of yellow sand. That is to say, there are areas of sparse scrub and trees, and sufficient herbage to support a certain amount of wild life, including big game, notably in the region of what is called the Etosha Pan. This is a vast low-lying area of what was once an inland sea but is now mostly black saline slime. There is a similar marshy piece of country called the Okavango Basin.

Living a homeless precarious existence on whatever they can kill, or dig up out of the ground, are small brown natives called Bushmen, perhaps the most primitive people left on earth. There is a theory that these were the prehistoric inhabitants of the whole of Central Africa. Harassed by Arab slave traders in the north, they were forced south. Then, to South Africa, came the white men, so the last remnants of the tribes finally found refuge in a land so barren and so

* Bechuanaland became the Republic of Botswana on 30th
September, 1966.

inhospitable that nobody wanted it. The Kalahari. There they learned to live practically without food or water, saved from extinction by a small melon, called T'Sama, which at certain times of the year grows in patches sometimes covering many acres. It provides both food and drink, and buried in the ground will keep for a long time.

The Bushman still lives the life of his remote ancestors, but it is likely that his days are numbered. His only weapon is a small bow which shoots a poisoned arrow. An animal struck by one will eventually die, but before it collapses the archer may have to follow it for days. He then eats as much as his stomach will hold: one might say more, because living as he does his stomach has developed the faculty of extraordinary expansion, so that he is literally pot-bellied. He has now, perforce, come to accept the white man.

Inevitably there are strange tales and rumours about the Kalahari, told by explorers or perhaps drift in through the Bushmen. One concerns the ruins of a lost city in the sand; of long man-made walls and terraces. There are tales of treasures, of course, some of fabulous deposits of diamonds in dried-up river beds. There may be some truth in these because from time to time a Bushman has produced a fine diamond. Where it came from he will not say. Perhaps he doesn't know. It may have accompanied the tribe through years of wanderings. As in other parts of Africa there have been rumours of a lost race of white men, isolated and cut off from civilization by hundreds of miles of desert. But maybe these can best be forgotten.

W.E.J.

CHAPTER 1

A NOBLE LORD IN TROUBLE

THE intercom telephone on Biggles' desk buzzed. He picked up the receiver. 'Bigglesworth here,' he said. After listening for a moment he went on: 'Right away, sir,' and replaced the instrument. 'The chief wants to see me,' he informed his staff pilots and left the room.

A knock on the door and he entered the office of Assistant-Commissioner Air Commodore Raymond, head of the Special Air Section at Scotland Yard.

'Have you had any report of a plane being lost, stolen or strayed from its hangar?' questioned the Air Commodore without preamble.

'No, sir. If anything like that happened we've had no information about it,' answered Biggles.

'I see. That answers that question.'

'Had you a reason to suppose that an aircraft was missing from its base?'

'It was just a possibility. Forget it for the time being. I've just had a visit from Sir Basil Goodall who, in case you don't know, holds an important job in the Diplomatic Corps. He thinks we might be able to help him – or rather, help a friend of his.'

'Who's the friend?' inquired Biggles, a trifle suspiciously.

'Lord Phillip de Langdon of Ferndale.'

Biggles smiled faintly. 'So we now move in high society.'

'Do you know anything about him?'

'Never heard of him.'

'Nor had I until this morning,' admitted the Air Commodore. 'Matter of fact, all I know now is what I have just learned from Sir Basil and gathered from a line or two about him in *Who's Who*.'

'And what have you learned, sir?'

'He's sixty-two, a widower with a daughter of sixteen and lives at Ferndale Manor, in Surrey. His hobbies are travel and big game hunting, a subject on which he has written one or two books. The title was created in the sixteenth century. That's about all. Four lines in *Who's Who* is a very short piece for a noble lord of ancient ancestry. I gather from Sir Basil that he's a bit eccentric, shuns publicity and doesn't take kindly to strangers.'

'That doesn't sound very promising. What's his trouble?'

'It appears he has lost some valuable property.'

'Consisting of what?'

'A collection of rubies, one reputed to be fabulous.'

'How did he lose them?'

'They were stolen.'

'From the house?'

'Presumably.'

'So the local police will be on the job.'

'No. They have not been informed of the theft.'

'Why not?'

'His lordship doesn't want a fuss. As I've said, he dislikes publicity.'

'That's a queer outlook. What does he expect us to do?'

'Find the rubies, I imagine. We shall know more about it when we've seen him.'

'Are we going to see him?'

'Yes. Right away. Sir Basil rang up from here and made an appointment for us for eleven-thirty.'

Biggles glanced at the clock. 'We haven't too much time.'

'That's all right. Ferndale Manor isn't far from Dorking. We should get there inside an hour.'

'Was there any reason why he shouldn't have come here?'

'I suppose there wasn't. Maybe there's something in the house he thinks we ought to see. Or perhaps as a peer of the realm he expects to be waited on. All I know is he got in touch with Sir Basil for advice and he must have decided that we were the best people to tackle the problem.'

'For any particular reason?'

'Apparently his lordship has reason to believe that an aircraft may have been used by the thief for his get-away. That's why I decided to take you along to hear the story at first-hand.'

'Ah! So that's where we come in. No doubt we shall find that the manor stands in a park with an open space big enough for a plane to land on.'

'No. That's the very question I put to Sir Basil. He knows the place and says it's all pretty well wooded.'

'Then I don't get it.'

'We shall learn more of the aviation aspect from Lord Langdon, no doubt.'

'When did this theft occur – yesterday?'

'It may have been anything up to two months ago.'

'*Two months!* For crying out loud!'

'The rubies were kept in a safe in the library. Lord Langdon rarely had occasion to look at them. Three days ago he decided, for some reason, to check them. They had disappeared.'

'So he doesn't know *when* they went?'

'No.'

'It could have been weeks ago?'

'Yes.'

'Then all I can say is he has a mighty poor chance of ever seeing them again. Why did he suddenly decide to check them?'

'I don't know. Perhaps he'll tell us. But let's be on our way. I have a car standing by.'

'Seems a queer business to me,' muttered Biggles. 'Do you mind if I use your phone to tell Lissie to take over as I'm going out?'

'Do so.'

Biggles put through the call and he and the Air Commodore went down to the car.

In a little over an hour it was cruising up a broad avenue of stately beech trees.

'These weren't planted yesterday,' observed Biggles.

'No. Nor the day before,' returned the Air Commodore dryly. 'As I told you, the Langdons have been here a long time.'

'I don't see anywhere here for a plane to get down,' said Biggles, looking around. 'Sir Basil was right. More isolated trees than open land.'

The mansion house, a big, sprawling but imposing building, came into sight. 'I wonder how his lordship gets the money to keep up a place of that size,' murmured Biggles. 'Most of these vast old houses are either falling down or being converted into flats or offices.'

'Maybe rents from the farms on the estate keep him going,' surmised the Air Commodore. 'Or, of course, he may have sold some of the outlying land for capital. I imagine Lord Langdon to be the sort of man who would hang on to the family home as long as possible.'

'Of course, if he ran short of money there would always be the rubies to fall back on – if he still had them.'

The Air Commodore looked at Biggles sharply. 'What does that imply?'

'Nothing ... nothing ... except that if his lordship was

reckoning on them as an asset he'd be shaken to find they'd gone.'

The Air Commodore looked at his watch. 'Just in nice time,' he said, as Biggles brought the car to a stop before the pillared front entrance.

The door bell was answered by an old man in the dress of a house servant. The Air Commodore gave his name.

'His lordship is expecting you, sir,' said the man gravely. 'He is waiting for you in the library. Follow me, please.'

A short walk down a corridor decorated with hunting trophies brought the little party to a door. A gentle knock and the manservant opened it to announce: 'Air Commodore Raymond, my lord.'

A man was standing alone on a tiger-skin rug in front of the fireplace below the mounted head of an African buffalo with a tremendous spread of horns. 'Come in,' he invited, in a deep sonorous voice which nevertheless had a hard edge on it. 'Pray be seated.'

'I've brought Air Detective-Inspector Bigglesworth with me,' said the Air Commodore. 'He's my chief aviation expert,' he explained.

'Good. Good. We shall need all the brains we can muster to solve this unpleasant problem,' said Lord Langdon, in his deep voice. 'Would you care for a glass of sherry after your journey?'

The offer was accepted, Biggles looking hard at the man they had come to see. He had half expected an unusual type but nothing quite as outstanding as this.

Lord Langdon would have been a striking figure anywhere, in any society. He was not less than six and a half feet tall with shoulders in proportion. With a figure as straight and lean as that of an athlete, he certainly did not look his age. The only indication of it was a few grey hairs in a bristling black beard. His hair, too, was thick, and worn rather long. The skin of his face, stretched tightly over the bones, had a parchment-like quality. It was dominated by a nose shaped like the beak of a bird of prey. Thick bushy eyebrows overhung dark eyes that had a disconcerting glint in them. As a young man he must have been strikingly handsome, decided Biggles. Whatever else he might be, this was not a man to be trifled with. He seemed to ooze energy, power, and inflexibility of purpose. He would have dominated any company.

He fitted well into the room in which he had received his guests. It appeared to be a mixture of library, museum and armoury. From all sides, above and around glass-fronted bookcases, were the heads of dangerous animals, white-fanged, red-mouthed, eyes glaring. The skin of what must have been a monstrous snake, a python or anaconda a full twenty feet long, ran almost the length of one wall. Biggles did not doubt that the man pouring out the drinks had been responsible for the deaths of all these creatures. He must have spent a great deal of his life doing it.

At intervals on a wall, resting on brackets, were the instruments that had done the killing; a regular battery of firearms, from shotguns to a variety of rifles which included an elephant gun. In a corner of the room, on a stand, looking rather incongruous, was a safe, a simple old-fashioned model which any safe-breaker who knew his job would have opened in five minutes.

Lord Langdon handed his guests their drinks with large sinewy hands which Biggles was sure could have tied an iron poker into a knot.

'I will tell you why I sought the advice of Sir Basil Goodall,' he said. 'He is one of my few friends, one of the very few men I would trust. Moreover, he knows my aversion to publicity. I trust that you, too, will respect my confidence. Let us have that absolutely clear from the outset. I want no word of this to get into the newspapers. I would like to recover the property I have lost, but I have no interest whatever in the thief. As far as I am concerned he can go to hell.'

'It would be impossible to convict this man, even if we caught him, without taking him to court; and if he is taken to court, the case would be heard in public and consequently reported in the press,' the Air Commodore pointed out.

'We will deal with that obstacle when we come to it,' was the answer. 'First I will tell you my story. When I have finished you may ask me any questions you wish and I will answer them to the best of my ability. Let us start at the beginning.'

Lord Langdon sat down.

CHAPTER 2

LORD LANGDON TELLS THE STORY

'I HAPPEN to be the owner of a fine collection of jewels,' began Lord Langdon. 'They are heirlooms. How much they would be worth in the open market today I do not know. To the best of my knowledge they have never been expertly valued. They were kept in that safe.' The speaker pointed to the safe in the corner. 'They are no longer there. When they were taken I do not know, but I think I know the man who took them.'

'But you must have *some* idea of when they disappeared,' the Air Commodore said.

'Why should I? I rarely had occasion to open the safe. Even now, but for the most extraordinary fluke, I would not have known that the jewels, which consist largely of a re-markable collection of rubies, had gone.'

'You reported the theft at once to the local police, of course.'

'No. I never do anything in a hurry. I felt I needed time to think about it.'

'The insurance people won't like that, sir.'

'The jewels were not insured.'

Biggles looked incredulous. 'Why not, sir?'

'It would have meant trouble; inventories, valuation and that sort of thing, and somehow I never found time to get around to it. You see, more often than not I am abroad. I can let you have a list of the items from memory should you need one.'

'The delay in reporting the theft won't make it any easier for us to recover your property,' said the Air Commodore dubiously. 'It could be anywhere by now. How were the jewels kept in the safe – in cases?'

'No. They were all rolled up together in a piece of black velvet. They were always kept like that even when my wife was alive. She seldom had occasion to wear them. My daughter has never worn them. She is not old enough. On my death they would have become hers.'

'She knew what was in the safe?' queried Biggles.

'Yes. One day, some time ago, I showed her the jewels.'

'You say you think you know who took them?'

'Yes. But I have no proof.'

'Whom do you suspect?'

'A man who was employed here: a footman named Richard Browning. It came about like this. About twelve months ago my old footman, Parker, who had served the house since he was a boy, died. I advertised in *The Times* newspaper for a new man to replace him. I had several replies, but the man I chose made his application in person. I liked him. He was a good-looking, well-spoken young fellow with an open, honest face, who looked you straight in the eye. As his references appeared to be in order I engaged him on the spot. For a long time I had no reason to regret this. He was intelligent above the average and it was remarkable the way he settled down to his duties. This is a big house, but he soon knew his way about as if he had lived here all his life.'

'You say his references *appeared* to be in order,' prompted Biggles. 'Weren't they?'

Lord Langdon picked up from the table some papers pinned together. 'Here they are. Bogus. Fakes, every one of them.'

'When did you discover this?'

'During the last day or two.'

'Didn't you check at the time?'

'No. I suppose that was careless of me. Rather than go to any trouble I accepted them at their face value.'

The Air Commodore shook his head sadly. 'You were asking for trouble. May I ask what caused you to go to the safe to check that the jewels were there?'

'That was most extraordinary. Last week I went to London to do some shopping. Walking down Bond Street I paused to look in the window of a jeweller's shop. Forniers, to be precise. Imagine my surprise when I saw offered for sale a ring identical with the one I had here: a large ruby set in a circle of diamonds. My first impression was that it must be a facsimile.'

'You didn't go into the shop to examine the ring closely, or ask the man how he had come by it?'

'No. You see, I wasn't absolutely certain that the ring was mine. That evening, when I got home, I went to the safe to refresh my memory. Judge my dismay when I found that not only was the ring missing but everything else.'

'What did you do?'

'I sat down to think about it.'

'You haven't been back to the shop?'

'No. I couldn't prove that the ring was mine: that it had been stolen.'

'So you came to the conclusion that the thief was your footman, Browning?'

'Everything pointed to it.'

'Such as, for instance?'

'He had gone. Disappeared.'

'Don't you know where he is?'

'I haven't the remotest idea. A month or so ago I had to speak to him rather sharply and he walked out on me. He must have taken the jewels with him.'

'What was the trouble?'

Lord Langdon hesitated. 'This is rather a delicate matter,

the chief reason why I have done nothing about the robbery. I would hate to have this made public, but it seemed that Browning was becoming too familiar with my daughter.'

'Could you be a little more specific, sir? What do you mean by familiar?'

'They were having secret meetings. I had noticed them exchanging glances, so I kept my eyes open. I came upon them whispering on the stairs. One evening I saw Lady Caroline, my daughter, leave the house by a side door and walk across to a shrubbery. I followed and found her talking to Browning. They could only have met there by appointment. No good can come of that sort of thing. Apart from the differences in their ages, my daughter is an heiress. Heiresses have, I am aware, been known to marry servants, but that sort of marriage seldom works out. Caroline is still only a girl, not yet seventeen, and I didn't want to see her make a fool of herself.'

'What did you do about this?' asked the Air Commodore.

'I sent for Browning and told him in no uncertain manner that this familiarity had got to stop.'

'What did he say to that?'

'He got on the high horse almost to the point of insolence. He said there had never been the slightest suggestion of intimacy with my daughter and never could be.'

'Did he say could, or would?'

'Does it matter?'

'It might. There is a distinction.'

'I think he said *could*.'

'What exactly did you take that to mean?'

'I don't know.'

'Does your daughter go out much?' inquired Biggles.

'Very seldom. What has that to do with it?'

'I was only thinking, it would be understandable for her to find someone to talk to, a companion, in the house.'

'Possibly, but I was not prepared to risk what that might lead to.'

'So you discharged him?'

'No. I warned him to remember his place and let it go at that.'

'Did he?'

'As far as I know, for the short time after that he remained with me. One morning he was no longer here and he has not been seen since.'

'Did he know what was in the safe?'

'I don't see how he could have known. I certainly didn't tell him.'

'But if he took the jewels he *must* have known they were there.'

'I cannot recall ever opening the safe while he was in the room.'

'How many keys of the safe are there?'

'Only one.'

'Who keeps it?'

'I do, although I don't actually carry it about with me. For the sake of convenience it is always kept in this thing.' The 'thing' to which Lord Langdon pointed was a small carved ivory box on the mantelpiece.

'Is the key still there?' asked Biggles.

'Yes.'

'Did Browning know the key of the safe was kept in that box?'

'Not unless he discovered it by accident, which seems unlikely, since he seldom had reason to work in this room.'

'Did your daughter know where the key of the safe was kept?'

Lord Langdon frowned. 'What does that imply? Are you suggesting that my daughter may have taken the jewels?'

'Certainly not, sir.'

'As they will one day be hers, it is hardly likely that she

would help a thief to take them by telling him where the key of the safe was kept.'

Biggles agreed that it did seem improbable. 'I am only trying to make sense of something which doesn't quite add up. Am I right in thinking that only you and your daughter knew what was in the safe?'

'Yes, to the best of my knowledge.'

'Have the jewels ever been exposed so that a professional thief would know the jewels were somewhere in the house?'

'Until they disappeared they hadn't been taken out of the safe for more than five years. The last time they were worn was by my late wife.'

'I see, sir,' said Biggles quietly. 'Let us change the subject. I was given to understand that somewhere, somehow, aviation came into this disturbing picture. Is that so?'

'Yes. Browning was an air pilot. He held a pilot's certificate.'

Biggles' eyebrows went up. 'Indeed! That is interesting. Did he do any flying while he was here?'

'Yes, I believe he did, although I have no definite information about it. When he applied for the vacancy here, he told me that aviation was his hobby and had been for a long time. One of the first things he did when he came here was join the Mealing Flying Club, which is also a flying school. It is only about twelve miles from here. He travelled to and fro on a motor-cycle. He went regularly on his day off. According to Stewart, my butler, all the books in his room were on aviation, navigation and kindred subjects. I understand they are still here. He didn't bother to take them with him when he left, so apparently he had no further use for them.'

'I'd like to see them sometime, if I may,' requested Biggles. 'They may provide a clue as to his whereabouts.'

'Whenever you wish. That can easily be arranged. Is there

anything else you would like to do while you are here?'

'I shall want a full description of this man Browning.'

'I can show you a photograph of him, although it is not a studio portrait.'

'That would be most helpful.'

Lord Langdon opened a drawer in the table and took out a small piece of paper, about four by three inches, evidently a photograph taken by an amateur. He handed it to Biggles who, when he looked at it, opened his eyes wide in undisguised surprise.

It showed a tall, dark, lean, good-looking young man in a bush shirt and shorts. In his hand, the butt resting on sandy ground, was a rifle. At his feet, stretched out to its full length, lay a dead leopard. Standing beside him was a short, ugly little man with a pot belly, clad only in a strip of rag in the form of an apron about his loins.

'So this is Richard Browning,' murmured Biggles.

'Without a doubt.'

'Would you say it is a recent photograph?'

'I'd say it was taken within the last two or three years.'

'He must have just shot the leopard.'

'Presumably.'

'Not the sort of pastime one would have expected of a footman.'

'That thought did not escape me.'

'What explanation did he give when he showed you this?'

'He didn't show it to me. It came into my hands after he had gone, and then only by an odd chance. I picked up a book my daughter had been reading to put it away. This picture, which had apparently been used as a bookmark, fell out.'

'And you kept it?'

'Yes.'

'You didn't mention it to her?'

'No.'

'Why?'

'I left it to her to ask me if I had seen it. That would have provided me with an opportunity to question her about it. But she has never mentioned it. Neither have I.'

'Browning must have given it to her.'

'I suppose so. What do you make of it?'

'Obviously Browning was not always a footman. This photograph was taken in a rarely visited part of South Africa; to be precise, in the Kalahari Desert.'

'How do you know?'

'The native is a Bushman. You won't find them anywhere else.'

'Have you been there?'

'Yes. Once. A long time ago.'

'You are quite right. This snapshot must have been taken in the Kalahari. Further proof is provided by the leopard The pattern of the markings are unique to the Kalahari. I can confirm that.'

'There was a third person present at the time; the man who held the camera. I think that's about all we can say about it. Did Browning ever mention to you that he had been to Africa?'

'No.'

Biggles passed the photograph on to the Air Commodore. 'I'm afraid this doesn't help us much,' he said. 'In fact, it merely extends the possible range of Browning's whereabouts.'

'As I said earlier, I'm not interested in Browning,' said Lord Langdon shortly. 'But I would like my rubies back.'

'You can't have one without the other,' returned the Air Commodore, dryly. 'There has been a robbery and it will have to be cleared up. We shall of course do our best to keep your name out of the papers.'

'Very well. Is there anything else you would like to do while you're here?'

'I would like to have a word with your daughter, alone, if you have no objection,' Biggles said. 'If that's all right with you, sir,' he added, to the Air Commodore.

Lord Langdon said, 'I have no objection, but you will learn nothing from her. She will not even discuss the matter with me.'

'She knows what has happened, of course.'

'She had to know.'

'She may talk to me, or she may let something slip. If she was sufficiently interested in Browning to accept this photograph she must know something about his background.'

'I agree; but if she knows anything she will not divulge it. She is in her sitting-room, where she now spends most of her time.'

'Does she seem very unhappy over the disappearance of Browning?'

'Curiously enough, not particularly.'

'In view of what you have told us, my lord, I would have thought she would be in a state of distress.'

'Nothing like that.'

'Hadn't you better ask her first if she will see me?'

'She would almost certainly refuse. If I show you in, taken by surprise she could hardly object without being rude. Come this way.'

CHAPTER 3

THE LADY CAROLINE

OUTSIDE, in the corridor, Lord Langdon stopped to tap gently on a side door. He opened it and entered. 'Ah, Caroline, there you are,' he said. 'I thought I'd find you here. I want you to meet Inspector Bigglesworth of Scotland Yard. He would like a few words with you.' Having said this, he brought Biggles in and then withdrew, closing the door behind him.

Biggles walked slowly forward, taking stock of the Lady Caroline Langdon. She was half sitting, half reclining on a settee, a magazine in her hands. There was nothing particularly remarkable about her. She was slight, as would have been expected from her age, with the dark hair and eyes of her father. She was attractive in a severe sort of way rather than pretty. She was dressed simply in a tweed skirt and polo-necked pullover. She did not move, but regarded her visitor with frank disfavour, meeting his eyes squarely.

Without waiting for Biggles to speak, she said: 'I don't want to appear discourteous, Inspector, but if you have come to ask questions you are wasting your time. I have nothing to say.'

'Does that mean you know nothing or *won't* say anything? '

'Take it which way you like.'

'Oh come, Lady Caroline, aren't you being rather hard on your father?'

'No harder than he is with me.'

'What does that mean?'

25

'We are out of sympathy.'

'You do not see eye to eye in certain matters, eh?'

'You can put it like that. You may sit down, but I hope you won't stay too long.'

'Thank you. You know why I am here?'

'I can imagine.'

'In view of what has happened, you could hardly expect your father to do nothing about it.'

'I don't care what he does. I'm not interested.'

'Even though the missing articles will one day become your property?'

'I don't want the jewels, if that's what you mean.'

'Then you must be a very singular young woman.'

'Perhaps I am. Is that all?'

'Not quite. You know, of course, that your father's ex-footman, Richard Browning, is suspected of stealing the jewels.'

'He did not steal them.'

'I was hoping you would help me to prove that; otherwise he will remain under suspicion all his life – or until he is caught. I am not here to condemn him but to try to arrive at the truth. If you would help me it might well be to his benefit.'

'There are facts in this case, Inspector, which you are never likely to guess.'

'Such as?'

'That is for you to find out.'

'By withholding what you know, you are doing both your father and Browning a grave disservice. You are obviously protecting Browning. Why?'

No answer.

'At least tell me this,' went on Biggles. 'It would explain your attitude. How far with Browning did your friendship go?'

'Quite a long way.'

'Let me put it bluntly. Were you, or are you, in love with him?'

A flicker of a smile softened Caroline's face. 'No. There could never be any question of marriage, if that's what you mean. Had that been possible, it is unlikely I would be here now. I would have run away with him. Does that shock you?'

'Not particularly.'

'We were just good friends.'

'Was he already married, perhaps?'

'No.'

'You're quite sure of that?'

'Quite sure.'

'You're being very mysterious.'

'Life is full of mysteries.'

'You're rather young to have discovered that.' Biggles smiled.

'I'm learning.'

'Do you know where Browning is now?'

'No.'

'Oh come on, Lady Caroline. Be frank with me. It could save everyone a lot of trouble. Are you asking me to believe that he has gone completely out of your life?'

'I'm not asking you to believe anything.'

'In your conversation with him he must have told you something about his past life.'

'Quite a lot.'

'About the time he spent in Africa, for instance?'

Her eyes opened wide at that, telling Biggles the shot had gone home. 'I never mentioned Africa,' she said sharply.

'No. I did.'

'Why Africa?'

'He had to live somewhere and it wasn't necessarily in England. You know his references were forgeries?'

'I know it now.'

'It suggests he had some particular reason for wanting to come here.'

'I suppose that is possible.'

'Was it because he knew what was in the safe in the library?'

'Really, Inspector! I'm not a thought-reader. How could I know what he was thinking? If you are trying to trap me I shall have to ask you to leave.'

'I'm sorry, Lady Caroline, but please try to realize that I am only doing my job. You have made it clear that you don't want to help me, so let us say no more about it. But sooner or later, with your help or without it, I shall learn the truth of this matter. The law has a long arm and an even longer memory. I think I ought to warn you of the possible consequences of being an accessory to a felony.'

'I accept the risk.'

'Did you yourself take the jewels from the safe?'

'No.'

Biggles stood up. 'Very well. Now I will leave you. Thank you for having received me, even though you haven't been what one might call co-operative.' He hesitated. 'Your decision in this matter is final?' he queried.

'What decision?'

'To protect Browning.'

'Would you betray a friend, Inspector?' she parried.

'That depends on what you mean by betray. I might, if I was convinced it was for his own good.' Biggles walked slowly towards the door.

'What are you going to do now?' she asked.

Biggles turned. 'I'm going to find Browning, of course.'

'I wouldn't give much for you chance, Inspector.'

'You may be surprised,' Biggles told her, and leaving the room returned to the library.

'Well, did you have any success?' inquired Lord Langdon, with a touch of asperity.

'In a negative sort of way, yes, sir.'

'What did she tell you?'

'It was what she declined to tell me that I found most informative.'

'What did she say about Browning?'

'Practically nothing. She refuses to be drawn.'

'Do you think she's in love with the rascal?'

'In my considered opinion, no.'

'Then why does she refuse to discuss him?'

'I don't know. There must be a reason. I have an impression there is, or was, an understanding between them; a sort of attachment, a bond if you like, which prevents her from saying anything that might be detrimental. I'm convinced that she knows more than she is willing to admit.'

'Do you think there is any likelihood of her running away to marry him?'

'I don't know what's in her mind, of course, but she assured me that she has no such intention. She was quite frank, and definite, about that. In fact, she assured me she *couldn't* marry him.'

'What do you take that to mean?'

'I don't know. I thought it might be because Browning was already married, but she said she was quite sure he was not.'

'Do you think she knows where he has gone?'

'That's difficult to say, but I fancy she has an idea.'

'Did you mention the photograph I found?'

'No.'

Lord Langdon paced up and down the room. 'I'm wondering if it wouldn't be better to let the whole thing drop,' he muttered irritably.

'And let Browning get away with it?'

'Yes.'

The Air Commodore stepped in. 'I'm afraid you can't do that.'

'Why not?'

'The matter is no longer entirely in your hands, my lord. A felony has been committed and the police are bound to take action.'

'Even if I make no charge?'

'That makes no difference.'

'What action will you take?'

'We shall continue to make inquiries in our own way and we shall rely on your co-operation. The first thing will be to ascertain if any more of your jewels have been sold. You have given me a list of the missing articles, so that should not be too difficult. Of course, if Browning has gone abroad, even if we find out where he is, it might be difficult to bring him home. Extradition is a long and involved process. But if Browning still has the jewels, it might be possible to recover them. That's really what you want, isn't it?'

'Yes. I don't care what happens to Browning.'

'This is assuming he is the thief,' put in Biggles. 'We don't know that for certain, so let's not prejudge him. Guilty or not, in view of their association here, I think it more than likely that Lady Caroline and Browning will sooner or later find a way of getting in touch with each other. How do your letters reach you?'

'They are delivered by the village postman.'

'Who is the first person to see them?'

'Whoever happens to answer the door bell. It might be one of the maids, or possibly my butler.'

'What about Lady Caroline?'

'It's unlikely that she would be down when the letters arrive.'

'Are you usually up and about at that time?'

'Yes. But I don't answer the door.'

'It might be a good thing if you did, for a little while.'

'You think Browning might try to correspond with Caroline through the post?'

'It is a possibility.'

'I see what you mean,' said Lord Langdon slowly. 'A letter addressed to her with a foreign stamp on the envelope . . .'

'Exactly. On the other hand, if Caroline knows where the man is, she might write to him to keep him informed of what goes on here. For instance, she might warn him that you have called in the police. But this again is supposing that Caroline is, or was, a party to the robbery.'

'The whole thing defeats me,' stated Lord Langdon wearily. 'Why on earth should Caroline help a thief to rob her own father, and in the long run, herself, as the jewels would one day have been hers? Very well, I will do as you suggest and keep an eye on the mail.'

'It would be significant if you suddenly found Caroline doing the same thing; it would indicate she expected a letter which she would prefer not to be seen by anyone else. All the same, for a girl who obviously has her wits about her, I find it difficult to believe that she would be so indiscreet as to allow Browning to write to her at this address. However, that seems to be as far as we can go for the moment.'

'Then you have no more questions to ask me?'

'Just one detail I would like to be clear on. On the day you went to London, and saw what you thought was your ring in a shop window, as soon as you got home you went to the safe?'

'That is correct.'

'And the key was in its usual place, in the box?'

'Yes. Otherwise I couldn't have opened the safe.'

'And you had no reason to suppose that it had been touched?'

'None whatever.'

'I see, sir. That settles that. May I keep this photograph of Browning for the time being? I will have a copy made and return the original to you.'

'Yes, you may do that.'

Biggles turned to the Air Commodore. 'That's all, sir, as far as I am concerned.'

The Air Commodore stood up. 'I have nothing more to say, so with your permission, Lord Langdon, we will be on our way. If there is any fresh development in this unfortunate affair no doubt you will inform me at once.'

'Of course. If I can be of any further assistance you have only to let me know. But remember, I don't want any mention of this in the newspapers.'

'I understand.'

Lord Langdon saw his visitors to the door and in a few minutes the police car was on its way back down the avenue to the main road. Out in the park some men were at work cutting down an oak tree. Biggles called attention to it.

'What about it?' said the Air Commodore.

'Nothing much, although it suggests his lordship hasn't as much money as one might suppose. A man in his position doesn't start selling his timber before he has to.'

'Hm. That's true,' agreed the Air Commodore. 'What do you make of it all?'

'Not very much, except that I have a feeling that someone isn't telling the truth, or, at all events, not the whole truth and nothing but the truth.'

The Air Commodore looked surprised. 'Why do you think that? I can understand the girl being difficult if she's infatuated with this fellow Browning, but surely there can be no reason why her father should withhold any relevant facts. He wants his jewels back.'

'Of course he does; but he seems desperately anxious for the whole thing to be kept under the hat. Why?'

'You tell me.'

'It's a guess, but I'd say there's something he hasn't told us, something he doesn't want to come out if some dirty linen has to be washed in public.'

'He gave us the reason.'

'Say *one* reason. He would have to provide one. There may be others. I'm keeping an open mind about that. I got the impression that if Caroline is trying to hide something, so is his lordship.'

'Naturally, he doesn't want a scandal over his daughter having a clandestine association with one of the male servants in the house.'

'That would be understandable,' conceded Biggles.

'What do you intend to do next?'

'Stop somewhere for lunch, I hope. Something inside me reminds me it's a long time since breakfast. There are two or three places in Dorking. After that, if it's all right with you, I shall go on to the airfield where Browning did his flying and have a chat with whoever is in charge. It used to be Bunny Hale. I met him in the war when he was with 104 Squadron, but he may have left. There's no need for you to come with me if you'd rather get back to the office. While we're having lunch, I could ring Bertie and ask him to bring down a spare car to take you back to the Yard.'

'Yes. We'll do that,' the Air Commodore decided.

'The next move will be to go to this jeweller in Bond Street, Forniers, and ask him how that ruby ring came into his hands. I can do that later.'

'We shall also have to check if any more of the missing pieces of jewellery have been sold; but that can be done through the usual routine channels. Lord Langdon gave me the complete list while you were talking to his daughter. What did you really think of her?'

Biggles shrugged a shoulder. 'A nice enough kid. I don't think she gets on too well with her father at the best of times. He strikes me as a hard, dominating character, and as she takes after him they're often in collision. I'd hate to work for him. You wouldn't get much mercy from him if anything went wrong. It's that streak in him, I imagine, that has caused him to spend most of his life going round the world killing things. I have never been able to understand the mentality of a man who delights in decorating his house with the heads of dead animals. It's a form of vanity, I suppose. It's as good as saying, I'm tough; look what I've done.'

'That's not our concern,' the Air Commodore said. 'We shall have to try to recover the stolen property.'

'That isn't going to be easy. First we have to find Browning and he might be anywhere. If he's gone abroad how are we going to bring him home?'

'We'll talk about that when you've found him. What are you going to do now?' continued the Air Commodore, looking surprised as Biggles brought the car to a stop in the village outside the shop-cum-post-office.

'I'm going to have a word with whoever runs the post-office here,' answered Biggles. 'I shan't keep you long.' He got out of the car and went into the shop. He was back in five minutes, a faint smile on his face. 'If there's any communication between Caroline and Browning it's through here it should come,' he explained. 'I've organized a double check in case the fair Caroline is too smart for her father. Now we'll press on and find a tavern to keep our strength up.'

CHAPTER 4

BIGGLES MAKES SOME CALLS

STOPPING at the first convenient restaurant, Biggles and the Air Commodore went in to lunch, Biggles first putting through a call to the office for a spare car to be brought down.

'What exactly did you do at the post-office in Ferndale?' asked the Air Commodore when they were at the table. 'You'd better tell me to keep me in the picture.'

'My chief reason for going in was to ask if any letters with foreign stamps had been noticed when the mail was being sorted for delivery. It's only a sub-post-office with a woman in charge. She handles all the mail. I didn't mention Lady Caroline, of course, or anyone at the manor, but as I see it, if his lordship is right about the relationship between his daughter and Browning, they'll try to keep in touch; and the only way would be through the post. Browning would hardly dare to come here, or use the telephone, not knowing who might answer the call. Contact will be made somehow. I can't see Caroline and Browning saying good-bye for ever and ever.'

'Why not?'

'Her behaviour would be different. She'd be upset. As it is she seems content with things as they are.'

'Had the postmistress noticed any foreign stamps? You're assuming Browning has gone abroad.'

'It seems more than likely, although we've no proof of it.

A letter for Caroline with a foreign stamp on it would be an indication. The post-woman could only remember one foreign stamp in recent weeks and that was for someone in the village named Smith. She didn't look closely at the stamp; she had no reason to; so she'd no idea of where it came from.'

'Did you make any arrangement with her to keep watch?'

'No. I merely said I'd call again.'

'Didn't she want to know the purpose of your questions?'

'Naturally. I had to tell her I was a police officer, but I couldn't say why I was making inquries without bringing Lord Langdon into it; and that I fancy would not have pleased his lordship had he got to hear of it. In any case, the postmistress has no right to interfere with the mail, so I wouldn't ask her to.'

'You're working on the assumption that Caroline and Browning will sooner or later get in touch through the post?'

'How else are we going to find out where he's gone? They may not be in correspondence at this moment, but Caroline will be anxious to tell Browning what's going on here. To do that she will have to know his address. She's on his side, there's no doubt about that, otherwise she'd talk instead of closing up like an oyster.'

Later, while they were still discussing the case Bertie arrived with a spare car. The Air Commodore, having paid the bill, took it over and departed, leaving the original car for Biggles' use.

'Where are we going?' asked Bertie, as they got in.

'Mealing aerodrome. It isn't far.'

'What's all the fuss about, anyway?'

On their way to the aerodrome Biggles gave Bertie a broad idea of what had taken him into the country.

'Seems all clear and straightforward,' observed Bertie, when he had finished. 'This bright lad Browning didn't like being ticked off by the old man, so he hoofed it, taking a few trinkets with him to settle the score. All we have to do when we get home is check on all the jewel thieves in the records.'

'It looks a bit *too* straightforward,' returned Biggles. 'These apparently simple cases have a trick of coming unstuck. I can see snags sticking out already. If Browning took those rubies he must have known the police would soon be after him, and sooner or later catch up with him. Why did he do it? If he had a crush on Caroline one would have expected him to stay around. Alternatively, why didn't Caroline go with him? There's something queer about the whole business. We shan't get any more out of Caroline, or his lordship, if, as I suspect, they're holding something back. I'm pretty sure Caroline knows the answers, but she's a shrewd young woman and she's decided to play it cool.'

'So what we have to do is find Browning.'

'That's it.'

'Do you expect to find him at Mealing?'

'No. But we may learn something about him. He has been doing some flying there; in fact, got his ticket; so there's just a chance he may have skipped in an aircraft.'

'But hold hard, old boy. If a plane had been pinched we'd have heard about it.'

'I'd have thought so. Of course, I may be on the wrong track altogether. But here we are. We shall soon know.'

Biggles turned into a lane which presently ended in a wide expanse of open country on which there were some buildings which included two hangars and a club house. Two men were working on a Tiger Moth. One of them was a small, dark young man with an outsize moustache. He looked round, staring, when Biggles hailed him with: 'Hello, Bunny. Still at it?'

Ex-Flying Officer Hale grinned broadly. 'Biggles, you old

perisher. Long time no see. What brings you here? Lost something?'

'No. Have you?' Biggles got out of the car.

'Not that I know of.'

'Good. That's really all I want to know. But as we're here we'll have a word. By the way, this is Bertie Lissie.'

'Come in and have a drink. What did you think I might have lost?'

'An aeroplane.'

'Nothing like that, thank goodness. Times are hard and we only have two, so if one had gone I'd have missed it. Take a pew. What'll you drink?'

'Nothing, thanks. We've only just had lunch. Tell me this. One of your members is a chap named Browning.'

'Say *was*. He isn't here now.'

'Do you know where he is?'

'Haven't a clue.'

'You taught him to fly and got him his ticket, I believe.'

'That's right.'

'What sort of pilot did he make?'

'Very good. Excellent. Never had a brighter pupil. Nice chap. Keen as mustard. I hope he's all right.'

'Any reason why he shouldn't be?'

'Well, you know how it is. He took off on a long-distance show and I haven't heard a word from him since.'

Biggles raised his eyebrows. 'But you said you hadn't lost a machine.'

'We haven't.'

'Then what machine did he take?'

'His own.'

Biggles frowned. 'His *own*. I don't get it. Do you mean he owned his own aircraft?'

'Sure. Why not? What's wrong with that?'

'Er – nothing, I suppose.' Biggles was still looking shaken. 'How did this happen?'

'Perfectly simple. A little while ago we bought a brand new *Martin*; twin-engined job; hoping to do some charter work. Browning flew it quite a bit. He seemed to have taken a fancy to it. Finally he took off in it for a long-distance trip.'

'What do you call long distance?'

'South Africa. He said he had a yen to beat the light plane record to Cape Town. When he started to get his papers together I offered to help him, but he said he could manage. It was all good practice. Said he'd have to learn how to get these things fixed up because he hoped to do quite a lot of flying. He had an extra tank fitted in the *Martin*. That's all. One morning he arrived here, as usual on his motor-bike, and away he went. That's all. I expected to have a line from him, but I haven't heard a word. He didn't tell me what I was to do with his motor-bike, so I half-expected him to come back here.'

'Did he take any luggage?'

'Only one of those light canvas bags handed out by the big air travel people.'

'Does he owe you any money?'

'Not a penny. He settled everything up to date before he left. He seemed to have plenty of money.'

'How did he pay for the *Martin*? By cheque?'

'No. In cash.'

'Didn't that strike you as odd?'

'Not particularly. Anyway, when I asked him why pay in cash, he laughed and said if he gave me a cheque it might bounce.'

'How much did he pay for the *Martin*?'

'Two thousand five hundred. That included fitting the extra tank, oil and fuel. Would you mind telling me what this is all about?'

'We're interested in him. That's all at the moment. Do you know where he lived?'

'Of course. He had to give us his address when he joined. He told me it was a temporary address. He was staying as a guest at Ferndale Manor.'

'Do you know anything about Ferndale Manor?'

'Not a thing.' Hale smiled. 'It seemed a good enough address. Don't tell me he's been a naughty boy.'

'We've no proof that he's been up to anything improper. I can only tell you that he left Ferndale Manor rather suddenly and unexpectedly; naturally, the people there are wondering what has become of him.'

Hale nodded. 'And no doubt his girl friend is thinking he may have had an accident.'

'Girl friend? What girl friend?'

'The girl he used to bring here occasionally on the back of his motor-bike.'

'A dark, slim girl about seventeen?'

'That's right. Do you know her?'

'I've met her. Did she do any flying here?'

'He gave her a joy-ride once or twice after he'd got his ticket. Nothing wrong with that, was there?'

'Not as far as I'm concerned.' Biggles got up. 'Well, I think that's about all. We won't keep you any longer. Nice to see you again. Oh! one last thing. Did Browning ask you to say nothing about him should anyone come here making inquiries?'

Hale shook his head. He looked surprised at the question. 'No. Why should he?'

'I thought there was a chance that he might. It isn't important. Anyway, he seems to have covered up his trail very smoothly. I'd be obliged if you'd let me know if you should hear from him. You know where to find me.'

'Scotland Yard, they tell me.'

Biggles nodded, smiling. 'We all have to earn a living somehow. Take care of yourself.'

'I'll do my best.'

'Happy landings.'

Followed by Bertie, Biggles went back to the car. 'So that's that,' he murmured as he drove away.

'You looked kind of shaken when Bunny said Browning had bought a plane.'

'I was. That was something I did not expect. Never gave such a possibility a thought. I have a feeling that Browning had all this very nicely planned.'

'Where could he have got the money, old boy? He'd hardly be able to save it out of his wages as a footman.'

'We may be able to find the answer to that.'

'Where?'

'At Forniers, the jewellers in Bond Street. As I told you, this whole thing blew up because Browning sold them a ring which Lord Langdon recognized as his. I imagine that would produce more ready money than Browning would need to buy the *Martin*. We shall see.'

Three quarters of an hour later the car was outside the shop in Bond Street. As there was no room to park, Biggles told Bertie to take it back to the Yard; he'd follow later in a taxi. Having seen the car drive on, he went to the shop front and looked through the window. It took only a moment to ascertain the first thing he wanted to know. The ring had not been sold. It was still there, unmistakable and conspicuous by being isolated from the rest of the objects offered for sale; a magnificent, large red stone, surrounded by small glittering diamonds. There was no price shown against it.

He went in. To the man who came forward to serve him he said, showing his police identification card: 'I would like to see the proprietor, or manager, if he's in.'

'Mr Fornier is in his office, sir. Just a moment.'

Within a minute Biggles had been conducted to the office of a man who said he was the owner of the establishment.

'I hope there's nothing wrong, Inspector,' he said anxiously. 'Please sit down.'

'Thank you. I would like to ask you one or two questions,' Biggles said. 'You have in your window a ring, a fine ruby set in diamonds. You will know the one I mean. It's exceptional. Is it yours?'

'Yes.'

'Will you please tell me how it came into your possession?'

'Certainly. It was brought to me by a man who wanted to sell it.'

'Did you know him?'

'No. I had never seen him before.'

'So you bought it.'

'Yes. But not there and then, of course. You should know, Inspector, that a shop with our reputation doesn't buy second-hand jewellery like that.'

'What did you do?'

'I told him that if he would leave the ring with me, and cared to come back in a week's time, I would have the ring valued and offer him a price. Actually, of course, this was to give me time to check with the lists of stolen property which are sent to me from time to time by the police. I could find nothing like it, stolen or lost. I rang up Scotland Yard for a double check.'

'Who did you speak to?'

'Inspector Gaskin. I have been able to help him once or twice. He had no record of the ring.'

'Quite right. He hadn't. The loss of the ring has only just been brought to our notice.'

Mr Fornier changed colour. 'I couldn't do more, could I?'

'No. You took all reasonable precautions. I assume this man said the ring belonged to him?'

'No. He was quite frank about that. He told me he was acting on behalf of a lady who wished to remain anonymous. She did not want it known that she was being forced to sell the ring to meet financial obligations. That is quite common these days.'

'You don't know the name of this lady?'

'No. In the circumstances I didn't ask him.'

'Did this man give you his name?'

'He had to; and his address; otherwise I would have had nothing to do with him.'

'What name did he give?'

'Browning. Mr Richard Browning. I have the address in my files if you want it. He asked me not to write to him there because he might be leaving any day. He would call back.'

'Was it, perhaps, Ferndale Manor?'

'Yes. That's right. I remember now you mention it.'

'What happened eventually?'

'He came back as arranged and I made him an offer for the ring. He accepted without quibbling.'

'How much?'

'Four thousand pounds.'

'How did you pay him – in cash?'

'Oh dear no. I don't keep that sort of money here. I gave him a bank draft payable to bearer. He cashed it later the same day. I know that because the bank manager went to the trouble of ringing me up to confirm that the cheque – a large amount – was in order. I said it was.'

'Have you seen this man since?'

'No.'

'He didn't try to sell you any more pieces of jewellery?'

'No.'

'Did he say he had any more?'

'No. I suppose he had just the one piece.'

'Would you recognize this man again if you saw him?'

'Yes.'

Biggles took the photograph of Browning from his wallet and showed it. 'Is this him?'

The jeweller answered without hesitation. 'Yes.'

'You're quite sure?'

'Absolutely. But tell me, Inspector. I'm getting worried. Is something wrong?'

'I'm sorry to have to tell you the ring was stolen.'

The colour drained from Fornier's face. 'Oh dear! This is a blow; one that looks like involving me in a heavy financial loss. But there, this is a risk we have to take, otherwise we'd do very little business. I would have sworn the man who sold me the ring was straight. He answered my questions frankly, and he certainly didn't look like a crook. Well, Inspector, I'm in your hands. What do you want me to do? I suppose you'll want to take the ring?'

'You can keep it for the time being until the question of ownership is definitely established. You'll have to take it out of your window. Keep it in your safe.'

'I will certainly do that.'

'Has anyone tried to buy it?'

'I have had offers, but nothing up to the figure I have been asking, which is four thousand five hundred pounds. A man is coming back tomorrow.'

'You'll have to tell him the ring has been withdrawn.'

'I'll do that. May I ask how you knew I had the ring?'

Biggles smiled sadly. 'Yes, I think I may tell you that. You were unlucky. The man who claims to be the owner of the ring, happening to pass your shop, noticed it in the window. Normally is was kept in his safe. He hadn't missed it. Well, I needn't keep you any longer. Mr Fornier. I'll leave the ring in your custody for the time being, but I may have to collect it later. Let me know if you see or hear any more of Mr Browning.'

'I will certainly do that.'

Biggles went out wondering if he had done the right thing in leaving the ring with the jeweller. However, there was no longer any chance of it being sold. He would speak to the Air Commodore about it. Even as he stood on the pavement waiting for a taxi, he saw it taken out of the window.

What he had learned threw some light on the case, but it puzzled him. On the face of what the jeweller had said Browning was undoubtedly the thief – unless he was really acting for Caroline; but why had he gone about the transaction so openly? Both at the aerodrome and at the jewellers he had used his real name. A professional thief would have used a false one. It looked as if he had suddenly wanted a large sum of money, so he had sold the ring. What about the other things? Why did he want the money? Was it to buy an aircraft? Why did he want a plane? Was it to make a quick get-away after the robbery? Where had he gone? Of one thing Biggles was convinced. This was no ordinary robbery. There was more behind it than had so far been revealed; or why was it that Lord Langdon merely wanted his jewels back and professed to have no further interest in the thief?

Biggles stopped a taxi and returned to his office at Scotland Yard.

CHAPTER 5

AN UNEXPECTED CLUE

THREE weeks had passed since the police had been called in, in somewhat unusual circumstances, by Lord Langdon, to solve the problem of the missing rubies. Since that day little progress had been made. Routine inquiries had continued, but no information had been received that the rest of the missing rubies had been offered for sale either at home or on the Continent.

Browning, the obvious thief – too obvious Biggles was inclined to think – had disappeared, perhaps literally, into thin air, to use the common expression. The course of his plane, where it had stopped to refuel, had been checked; Casablanca, Dakar, Brazzaville, so it looked as if he had really gone to South Africa, his avowed objective before departure, using the West Coast route. Why the West Coast, Biggles wondered. The East Coast is more usual. It was after Brazzaville that the *Martin* had disappeared. Beyond that there was no further news. He had not arrived in Cape Town. What had he done, or what had happened to him? Had his plane let him down, leaving him stranded in some remote spot with a fortune in jewels on board? Or had he deliberately flown to some outlandish place where he could quietly bury himself until the rubies were forgotten? Either could have happened. Biggles was inclined to the former theory, because otherwise the robbery would appear to have been pointless. A pocketful of rubies would not be much use in the middle of Africa.

There was, Biggles thought, one possible clue to where

Browning might have gone. Somewhere in the region of the Kalahari Desert. He must know something of the country because he had apparently shot a leopard there.

Biggles went in to see the Air Commodore about it – not for the first time. He said: 'Whether he's crashed, or simply gone to ground, we're not likely to hear any more of him for a long time, if ever.'

The Air Commodore agreed. 'What can we do about it?' he asked helplessly.

'There's only one thing left to do as far as I can see,' returned Biggles. 'And that is for somebody to follow his track and try to locate his plane, either intact or in small pieces.'

'That seems a pretty hopeless proposition.'

'I wouldn't say that, sir. Lost planes have been found. An aircraft isn't an easy thing to dispose of, or hide. Even if you burn it you leave a mess. Sooner or later somebody stumbles on it. Even natives talk.'

'That's true. Would you like to have a go at it?'

'That's up to you, sir. I will if you want me to.'

'All right. Go and see if you can find any sign of him or his plane. I'll get your papers ready. Take someone with you in case of accidents.'

'Okay, sir. I'll do that.'

Biggles had started making his arrangements the following day when the Air Commodore sent for him.

'I don't know quite what to make of this, but I've just had a phone call from Lord Langdon,' informed the Air Commodore. 'He says he has something to say, but he would rather not talk on the phone for fear of being overheard. I can't get away myself as I have a meeting presently, so perhaps you'll run down to see what this is about. Something must have turned up.'

'I'll do that right away, sir,' Biggles said. 'You might let his lordship know I'll be with him in about an hour.'

A little under an hour later he was cruising quietly through the main street of Ferndale village, although as a matter of detail, the village, like many villages, consisted of little more than one long straggling street. Observing that he had a minute or two in hand, he called at the post-office to check from the postmistress if she had noticed, by the stamps, if there had been any letters for the Manor from a foreign country.

No, he was told, there had been only one letter from abroad in the mail. It had come in that morning and had been delivered. It was an air mail letter for Mrs Smith. Nothing else. Who Mrs Smith might be he did not bother to inquire. He went on his way, turned in the drive to the Manor and presently was being shown into the library, the same room as before. Lord Langdon was waiting for him.

'I'm sorry to bring you down here again, but I am a little puzzled and I think you should know why,' he began. 'There may be nothing in it, but one never knows,' he went on in his deep voice. 'I could only use the telephone at the risk of being overheard; not necessarily by Caroline, but the servants, and they talk among themselves. I don't want any tittle-tattle in the house.'

Biggles nodded understandingly.

Lord Langdon continued. 'I think you should know that my daughter has taken to doing something unusual. Nearly every morning she goes out for a walk. She is away for anything up to two hours. As this is something quite new, I feel there must be a reason for it. Sometimes she walks down the drive as if she was going to the village; sometimes she takes a footpath through the woods.'

'Don't you know where she goes?'

'No.'

'You haven't followed her?'

'Certainly not.'

'And you haven't asked one of your staff to watch her?'

'Ask one of my servants to shadow my daughter! I wouldn't dream of doing such a thing,' declared Lord Langdon indignantly.

'I'm sorry, sir, but in the circumstances it seemed pardonable, and the easiest way to set your mind at rest.'

Lord Langdon fixed his penetrating eyes on Biggles' face. 'Do you suppose she can be meeting Browning in the woods, or somewhere?'

Biggles shrugged. 'Without a hint of what she's doing, I wouldn't like to make a guess; but from what I know, although that isn't much, in my opinion the possibility that she is meeting Browning is remote. It would surprise me if he was still in this country, never mind Ferndale. Do I understand you have taken no steps whatever to find out what she's doing?'

'Yesterday morning I made a point of being on the drive when she went out. Incidentally, she left the house by a side door, not the front door which she would use in the ordinary way.'

'You got the impression she went out that way in order not to be seen?'

'What else? However, making it appear accidental, I intercepted her and asked her, casually, where she was going. She said that as it was a fine day she was going to walk as far as the village shop to get one or two small things she required.'

'That sounds reasonable to me,' put in Biggles.

'It may, but it doesn't sound reasonable to me,' stated Lord Langdon crisply. 'Why should she suddenly make a practice of doing this? Why not take the car as she has in the past? Someone from the house goes to the village nearly every day to do any shopping that is necessary. If it comes to that why not use the telephone? An errand boy would deliver the things. No, there's something behind this.'

'I take your point, sir.'

'Caroline is out again today. What can she want now?'

'The shop is also the post-office. Can that be the attraction? Can she be going to the post-office to collect a letter?'

'That thought occurred to me, but the post-office is not her objective.'

'How do you know?'

'Allowing her plenty of time to get to the post-office, making the excuse I wanted Lady Caroline to bring me some stamps, I rang the post-office and asked if she was there. She was not. She had not been in. What is she doing?'

'You watched the mail as I suggested?'

'Yes. To the best of my knowledge she has not received a single letter since you were last here.'

Biggles got up. 'I see, sir. You were right to tell me this. I shall soon know what she's doing.'

'Does that mean you'll follow her?'

'Not me, personally. She knows me by sight. We have ways of doing these things. Leave it to me, sir.'

With that Biggles left the Manor.

Within a minute, after turning out of the drive into the village street, he saw the very person who had been the subject of his conversation with Lord Langdon. His daughter. The Lady Caroline. She was just leaving by the garden gate, an attractive, old thatched cottage, waving good-bye to a grey-haired woman who was standing in the doorway. For this reason she did not see him. Turning his head away instantly, he did not stop. But he allowed the car to drop to a crawl. Watching in the reflector he saw the object of his interest walk on briskly towards the Manor drive, apparently on her way home.

As soon as she was out of sight Biggles stopped his car and lit a cigarette to do some thinking. What he had seen, he thought, needed some serious consideration. He was still sitting there when a boy came along, apparently a village boy, whistling as he kicked an old tennis ball in front of him.

Biggles called him over. Speaking through the open window of the car, he said: 'Tell me, laddie, do you know who lives at the old thatched cottage that stands by itself a little way up the street?'

'Mrs Smith,' was the instant reply.

'Has she lived there long?'

'As long as I can remember. Why?'

A trifle disconcerted by the frank question, Biggles answered: 'I've been hoping to buy an old cottage like that.'

'Well you won't buy that one.'

'Why not?'

'It belongs to the Manor.' The boy continued on his way, whistling.

Biggles sat still for a minute, pondering what he had just heard. Then he cruised on to stop again at the post-office. He waited a little while until the shop was empty; then he went in and said: 'I'm sorry to trouble you again, but you told me there was an air mail letter for Mrs Smith.'

'Yes.'

'The old lady who lives at the thatched house.'

'That's right. Sunnyside.'

'I don't know the name of it. I believe that isn't the first letter with a foreign stamp you've delivered there.'

The postmistress frowned. 'I don't know that I'm right in answering these questions,' she said dubiously.

'It's your duty to help the police,' Biggles answered. 'Don't worry. This is strictly between ourselves.'

'If you say so. There's been one letter before, like I told you.'

'The one that came this morning. Could you see where it came from?'

'No. The stamp was smudged and nearly blotted out by the postmark. All I could see of the postmark was the first four letters. They looked to me like Wind – W-I-N-D.'

'Is Mrs Smith in the habit of having letters from abroad?'

'Never till lately, that I can remember.'

'Has she lived here long?'

'Ever since her husband died, some years ago. At one time they both worked at the Manor. He was a gardener and she acted as nursemaid to young Lady Caroline. When her husband died, as she was getting on a bit, his lordship let her have the cottage, rent free, I believe.'

'Has Lady Caroline been in the shop this morning?'

'No, I haven't seen her.'

'I see. I think that's all, thank you. Now you can help the police by forgetting I've been here asking questions. Say nothing to anybody – understand?'

'I understand. I hope it's nothing serious.'

'Nothing for you to worry about. You'll probably hear no more about it. I may have to look in again, but that's enough for now. Good morning.'

Biggles went back to his car with a faint smile of satisfaction on his face. Taking his seat, he lit another cigarette. The picture, or one side of it, was becoming clear. Where Mrs Smith stood in it was fairly obvious. She was acting as a go-between, probably in all innocence, between Browning and Lady Caroline. Browning wrote to the cottage. Caroline collected the letters. Mrs Smith had been Caroline's nursemaid. What more natural than her willingness to co-operate with Caroline, even if she didn't know what was going on?

Biggles' immediate problem was whether or not to tell Lord Langdon what he knew; that his daughter and Browning were in touch through a cottage in the village. If he reported what Mrs Smith was doing it might result in the old lady being turned out of her house. He didn't want that to happen. On the other hand, if he remained silent his lordship might discover the truth for himself, and that would probably do more harm than good. There would be a first-class row, which might end in Caroline running away to join Browning wherever he might be. Things were better as they were.

After giving the matter some careful thought, Biggles decided to put his lordship's mind at rest about his fears of Caroline meeting Browning in the locality. Mrs Smith need not be mentioned. With this intention he headed back for the Manor.

On the drive, not unexpectedly, he overtook Caroline on her way home. He slowed down. 'Can I give you a lift?' he asked through the open window.

Caroline continued walking, looking straight ahead. 'No thank you. I prefer to walk.'

'So you haven't changed your mind?'

'About what?'

'Do I have to tell you? It's usually good policy to trust the police.'

'If the police would mind their own business it would be better for everyone,' she retorted.

'Have it your way,' sighed Biggles, and drove on.

He reached the house some distance in front of her. 'Will you tell Lord Langdon I'm sorry to trouble him again, but I won't keep him a moment,' he told the butler who answered the door.

A minute later he was again shown into the library. Lord Langdon's dark eyes asked a question.

Biggles said, 'I've only come back to tell you, sir, that you need have no fear that Lady Caroline is in personal contact with Browning, either here or anywhere else.'

'It didn't take you long to work that out,' answered Lord Langdon curtly. 'How can you be sure?'

'I have good reason to believe Browning is abroad.'

'And what am I supposed to do?'

'If you'll be advised by me, sir, you'll do nothing. It would make my task easier if you'd leave everything to me.'

'Does that mean I'm to ignore Caroline's sudden passion for walking?'

'Yes. Take no notice.'

'Do you know what she's doing?'

'I think so.'

'What is she doing?'

'I'd prefer not to answer that question until I've confirmed that I'm right. That shouldn't take long. I can assure you she's doing no harm. To interfere at this stage might make things more difficult for me.'

'You're making this sound all very mysterious!'

'I'm sorry, sir, but I'm acting for the best. I can't promise to recover your rubies, but I have every hope of finding out where they went.'

'Very well, if that's how you want it,' said Lord Langdon gruffly.

Biggles took his departure and, returning to the Yard, went straight to the Air Commodore. 'His Lordship is worried because his daughter has taken to going for long walks by herself. I've been able to assure him that he has nothing to worry about.'

'Did you find out what she was doing?'

'She's in touch with Browning by post, but the letters from him are being delivered to an old woman in the village who was once a nursemaid at the Manor. Caroline collects them. I haven't told Lord Langdon this for fear of starting a rumpus.'

'Anything else?'

'Yes. The letters are coming air mail from Africa. The nearest the woman who runs the post-office could get to the postmark was the first four letters: a town beginning with

W-I-N-D. That looks as if it might be Windhoek. It's the only place I know in South-West Africa.'

'On the edge of the Kalahari Desert. Could that be a co-incidence?'

'Perhaps. Perhaps not. I was thinking on the same lines.'

'Might be a good place to start making inquiries.'

'I intend to make that my first objective.'

'Right. Then see what you can make of it. Who will you take with you – Lacey?'

'No. He's pretending to be fit, but I can see he hasn't fully recovered yet from the crack-up he had in India.* He's all right at home, but Africa might be a different story. If it's all the same with you I'll take Bertie Lissie.'

'As you wish,' agreed the Air Commodore. 'It's your party.'

'Just one last query, sir. What shall I do about Browning if I should happen to catch up with him? I can't bring him home.'

The Air Commodore considered the question. 'No,' he said pensively. 'I shall have to leave that to you. Try to find out what he did with the rest of Lord Langdon's jewellery. Better still, if he still has it, try to make him hand it over. If he cuts up rough the South African police might help you; but it would be better to work on your own, if you can, to avoid complications. It depends on what Browning is doing. It might be something illegal. But the first thing is to find him.'

'We should be able to do that, sir. A man with a private aircraft can't get far without somebody noticing him. Sooner or later he needs stuff called petrol, and I doubt if he'll find any in the Kalahari.'

With that Biggles left the room and returned to his own office.

* See Biggles in the Terai.

CHAPTER 6

THE TRAIL PETERS OUT

TEN days after the events recorded in the previous chapter, Biggles, with Bertie beside him in the cockpit, was winging his way down West Africa in the Air Police *Merlin*, the twin-engined, eight-seater aircraft, issued in the first instance for the special long-distance work in the Middle East narrated in *Biggles' Special Case*.

Following the usual route, so far all had been straightforward, stops having been made to refuel at the aerodromes and airports on a course to the Cape. At most of these they had found records of Browning's call nearly a month earlier. This told them nothing they did not already know beyond confirming what had been suspected. As in all his previous transactions, Browning had made no attempt to hide his trail, although, as a matter of fact, in an aircraft it would have been difficult for him to do so. He had paid cash, in the appropriate currency, for fuel, oil and accommodation. His papers were in order and he had cleared Customs in the usual way, saying he had nothing to declare, and this had apparently been the case. There had been no trouble anywhere. Clearly, the runaway footman had made his plans carefully.

As Biggles had more than once remarked to Bertie as without haste they continued on their course, there was one queer aspect to this. If Browning had the stolen rubies hidden somewhere in his aircraft he was taking a chance. Had he been caught in the act of smuggling precious stones, not only would the jewels have been confiscated, but he would ave been heavily fined, if not given a prison sentence.

'We should look daft coming all this way for nothing if he
idn't take the stuff with him after all,' observed Bertie.

'I suppose there is just a chance that he hid the rubies in
ngland, in a safe deposit or something of that sort,' re-
urned Biggles. 'But in that case, why steal them in the first
lace? Unless of course this rushing away in an aircraft was
nly a blind, and he intends to return to England as soon as
e thinks it's safe. He must have known that suspicion was
ound to fall on him as soon as the rubies were missed, and
hat was certain to happen eventually.'

'Maybe he thought that might not happen for weeks, pos-
ibly months, as would probably have been the case if Lord
Langdon hadn't spotted his ring in the shop in Bond Street,'
Bertie said. 'At all events we know he was the thief because
le sold the ring. The man who owned the shop recognized
im from the photo.'

'True enough,' agreed Biggles. 'But there's still something
which to my mind doesn't seem to fit. I can't decide whether
Browning is a fool to leave his trail wide open – or has he
een clever? Then again, there's the attitude taken by Caro-
ine. Why should she take sides with a man who robbed her
wn father, particularly as the jewels would one day have
een hers? As they're still in correspondence, she must
now where he is. What sort of nonsense is this?'

'The answer to that sticks out a mile,' declared Bertie.
'Whatever she says, she's still in love with the feller. When a
girl of her age gets this love fever she gets it badly, and is
capable of doing the daftest things.'

'You may be right, at that,' conceded Biggles, moodily.
'Then there's this extraordinary reluctance of Lord Langdon to have any publicity. Here's a man who has lost a
fortune in jewels, yet he doesn't want any fuss made about
it. Why? There must be a reason.'

'Obviously, he doesn't want a scandal involving his

daughter and a footman.'

'That's what he says; but I have a feeling that somewhere in the background there's a better reason than that.' Biggles looked down. 'We're getting over desert country, so keep your fingers crossed. This part of South-West Africa has an ugly reputation. Thirst has killed a lot of people here. Shipwrecked mariners coming ashore on the coast have died from want of water.'

'Is this the Kalahari under us?'

'No. That's farther to the east. By my reckoning we should see Windhoek in about an hour. I shan't be sorry. Keep your eyes on the ground for anything that looks like an aircraft in case Browning had to make a forced landing on his way south.'

'If he posted a letter from Windhoek he must have got there, old boy,' Bertie pointed out.

'Unless he got someone to post a letter for him; not very likely, I must admit.'

'Are you expecting to find Browning in Windhoek?'

'I'm hoping. If he isn't there, goodness knows where he might be. We're in a big country. Of course, he might have gone on to Cape Town. If he's in Windhoek, someone should have seen him. The place isn't all that big. We may find the *Martin* there. There's not likely to be another machine of that type in this part of the world. At all events, we shall know if he got as far as this. There's nowhere else, as far as I know, until Keetmanshoop, between three and four hundred miles farther on. So far the trail has been wide open. We know he topped up, as we did, at Nova Lisboa, in Angola, so all was well with him as far as that.'

'And having found him, what then?'

'I shall ask him point blank to cough up the rubies. There's nothing else we can do.'

'He'll refuse.'

'In that case we shall have to put our cards in front of the police in the hope of persuading them to put the screws on him to make him talk. If that fails, if they won't issue a search warrant, we shall have to do what we can on our own. But that looks like Windhoek coming up ahead. Let's see about getting in. Keep your eyes open for Browning's *Martin*. It may still be here.'

Twenty minutes later, having received permission to land, Biggles was on the ground, taxiing into the position ordered by the ground control officer. There were only four machines in sight, the most conspicuous being a Boeing of South African Airways. If the *Martin* was there it was not in view. Biggles switched off.

The next quarter of an hour was occupied by the usual formalities. These completed, they walked to the administrative buildings where Biggles asked to be directed to the office of the Airport Manager. Presently he found him at his desk, engaged with a man who turned out to be the Traffic Superintendent.

'What can I do for you?' asked the Manager.

Biggles showed his Scotland Yard credentials. 'We've flown out from London hoping you'll be able to help us,' he said. 'I'm looking for an aircraft and the man who was flying it; solo, I believe. The machine was a *Martin*. We've tracked it as far as here. Do you know anything about it?'

The Manager nodded. 'Sure. I remember it. It was here two or three weeks ago. Nice little twin-engined job.'

'You say *was* here. Does that mean it isn't here now?'

The Traffic Superintendent answered, 'It was only here a couple of days. Then it went on.'

'Do you know where the pilot was making for?'

'No. I imagined he was making for Cape Town.'

'Do you know if he got there?'

'No, but I could check.'

'I'd be obliged if you would. It might save me a long run for nothing.'

'I'll do that right away.' The Traffic officer went out.

Biggles continued talking to the Manager. 'Do you recall the name of the pilot?'

'Yes. Feller named Browning.'

'Did you know him?'

'I can't exactly say I know him, but I've seen him in the town once or twice. That was some time ago. Must be at least twelve months. The last I saw of him he was inquiring about a passage to England. What's wrong? Has he been up to something?'

'That's what we're trying to find out. We think he could tell us what we want to know – if we could find him.'

The Traffic Superintendent came back. 'They know nothing about a *Martin* at Cape Town.'

'What do you take that to mean?' asked Biggles.

'Well, obviously he didn't go there.'

'He may have run into trouble on the way.'

'You're talking about a chap named Browning?'

'That's right.'

'He may have gone out of his way to call on a pal of his in the Kalahari.'

Biggles stared. 'A pal? In the Kalahari?'

'Yes. Matter of fact I understood he was in partnership – sort of – with Mick Connor.'

'Who's he?'

'He's a cat man.'

'Cat man?' Biggles went on, 'I don't want to take up too much of your time, so to save me asking a lot of questions, it might be as well if you'd tell me what you know about Browning and Connor.' Biggles produced his photograph of Browning with the dead leopard. 'Let's get this straight. Is this the man Browning we're talking about?'

'That's him,' said the official, after a glance. 'Got a cat with him, too.'

'I get it. The cat being a leopard.'

'That's right. You ask about Mick Connor. He's been in these parts for as long as anyone can remember. He came here when the country was really tough, prospecting for diamonds, I understand, in the Kalahari. He didn't find any diamonds, so to keep himself in a grub stake he became a skinner; in other words, he shot big cats for their hides – lions, leopards and so on. Leopard skins fetch a lot of money, and now there aren't as many as there were, they become more and more valuable. Connor dried the skins and packed them off to an agent in Cape Town. When the railway came he put them on the train. Now he sends them by air. Trundles in, once in a while, in an old jeep he picked up somewhere. Most people know him by sight. He's a type you wouldn't easily forget. He stands about six foot six and has a hell of a scar right down his face where he got mauled by a cat some time. He must be getting on for seventy, although you wouldn't think it to look at him. Where he picked up Browning I don't know, but one day – some time ago – they rolled up in Windhoek together. They seem to have been together ever since. From time to time they'd roll up with a load of skins, do some shopping and disappear again.'

'Into the Kalahari?'

'So I suppose. It's as well not to ask questions of a man like Connor.'

'Has he some sort of headquarters, a dwelling of sorts, in the desert?'

'I wouldn't know.'

'Where would I be most likely to find him?'

'I wouldn't know that, either. There was a time I would have said probably somewhere near the Etosha Pan, because that's where most animals would be; but now the Pan is a Game Park, one of the places they show tourists. There is this about it. Mick Connor must know the Kalahari better than any living man. No doubt he's still hoping to

strike diamonds, but he'll have to be where there's game t
get his skins. That's as much as I can tell you. I haven't see
him lately.'

'You think there was a time when Browning was workin;
with him?'

'They used to come into Windhoek together, so what els
could he be doing? This was before Browning went to Eng
land, of course.'

'You must have been surprised when he came back her
flying his own plane?'

'I was. Naturally, I assumed he'd packed up with Connor
It even struck me that they'd made a rich find and gone their
own ways.'

'And you know nothing about Browning's background?'

'I've told you as much as I know. The first time I saw him
was when he rolled up here with Mick Connor.'

'I see. Thanks.'

'There's always a chance that he may come into Windhoek; but if you've any ideas of looking for him in the Kalahari, all I can say is you've got a job on your hands.'

'Having come so far, I might as well stick around for a
bit, if my machine won't be in your way.'

'That's all right.'

'Meanwhile we'll take a walk and find quarters where we
can think things over,' decided Biggles, getting up. 'I'll let
you know where we are. Then, if you should see either
Browning or Connor, you might let me know.'

'I'll do that. But if you take my advice you'll be careful
what you say to Connor if you should see him. He has a
reputation for having a hell of a temper. Remember, he's
Irish, and when he has a skinful of whisky he goes fighting
mad.'

'I'll keep it in mind,' said Biggles, as he and Bertie went
out.

'Well, so far so good,' remarked Biggles as they walked away.

'I don't see much good about it, old boy,' replied Bertie dubiously. 'We still don't know where this bounder Browning has gone.'

'I hardly expected to find him waiting here on the tarmac,' returned Biggles. 'At least we've proved our suspicions. We know he came to Windhoek. And we know he didn't go on to Cape Town. We've also learned he's been associated with a hunter in the Kalahari, so it would be fairly reasonable to suppose he came out here to rejoin him. He would probably know where to find him.'

'Does this mean we now have to start searching this pershing desert?'

'Unless we're content to sit here twiddling our thumbs for weeks, maybe for months, waiting for him, or his pal Connor, to come into the town for stores. Tomorrow, or as soon as we've fixed up quarters and had a rest, we'll have a look at the country east of here: this much talked of Wilderness. If, as they say, there are wild animals, it shouldn't be too bad.'

'But here, I say, dash it all, it's a pretty big area to start searching for an odd white man.'

'We've more than a man to look for,' reminded Biggles. 'Somewhere there should be an aeroplane, which is somewhat larger, and as there can't be many about in the Kalahari, we should be able to spot it. But before we go into details let's find somewhere to park our small-kit.'

They walked on.

CHAPTER 7
THE KALAHARI

IT did not take long for Biggles and Bertie to find the sort of accommodation they wanted, and having settled in, decided to have an easy day while the *Merlin* was given a top over haul. The following morning found them in the air with no other immediate object than to make a preliminary reconnaissance to see the country and pick out useful landmarks.

There had been one incident. As they were about to leave the hotel for the airport, they had a visitor; a sun-tanned young man dressed in the dark blue jacket and light blue trousers of the South African police. Having queried Biggles by name, he said: 'I'd like a word with you if you don't mind.'

'Go ahead,' invited Biggles readily.

'We heard you'd arrived and it didn't take us long to find you. Things being as they are, we like to know what strangers are doing,' explained the police officer. 'People give all sorts of reasons for coming to our part of the world, and those they give are not always the true ones.'

'I understand that,' Biggles said. 'How did you know we'd arrived in Windhoek?'

'From Mr Grey.'

'Who's he?'

'The Airport Manager. He lets us have the list of new arrivals. It is correct that you're detectives from London and that you're interested in Mick Connor?'

Biggles and Bertie showed their police papers. 'I'm only

64

interested in Connor in as far as I'm told he's a friend of a man named Richard Browning. He's really the man I want to see.'

'May I ask why you're looking for him?'

'We think he may have been implicated in something that happened when he was in England recently. Have you anything against him?'

'Not a thing. But we've had word from a private source that he's been seen flying over the Kalahari in the plane he brought back with him. Naturally, we'd like to know just what he's doing.'

'Why not ask him?'

'We would if we knew where to find him. He hasn't been back here since he left.'

'Have you any reason to suppose he's doing something irregular?'

'If he's with Connor he might be. For some time there's been a whisper that Connor's been shooting game on the fringe of, if not actually in, the reserve. We know he's a professional hunter. That's in order; but we don't like the idea of hunting game from a plane, if that's what he's doing. Not even ostriches.'

Biggles looked surprised. 'Why the devil should he go out of his way to shoot ostriches?'

'For diamonds.'

'*Diamonds!* I don't get it.'

'Some years ago a hunter in the Kalahari shot an ostrich. Having heard that ostriches swallow pebbles to digest their food, out of curiosity he examined its crop. What he found, among other things, was a diamond. Several, in fact. That was bad luck for the ostriches. It started a new kind of diamond rush – shooting ostriches. By the time people realized that not many of the birds carried diamonds, only those that had apparently wandered into the Kalahari from where there was diamond-iferous gravel, they were pretty well wiped out. However, some were left, and they're on the increase again. Maybe it'd be easy to shoot 'em from a plane if that's the game.'

'I see what you mean,' said Biggles thoughtfully.

'Talking of shooting,' went on the officer, 'are you carrying guns?'

'Just pocket automatics in case of emergency. We don't expect to use them.'

'Have you got permits?'

'Yes, they were issued by your London office. We declared them at the airport. By the way, these Bushmen. I understand there's nothing to fear from them!'

'Oh no. They're tame enough nowadays. They've learnt that white men usually have food. Give them some grub and they won't stop eating till they've finished it. To them there's only one safe place to store it – in their bellies.' The policeman hesitated. 'You'd better be careful, though.'

'Why?'

'We've heard a rumour that Connor has been treating some of the natives a bit rough, and they may be in a resentful mood. If that's true, he must be a fool and may live to regret it. One day one of their poisoned arrows may come his way. The poison may be slow and take days to kill, but the end is a foregone conclusion. The stuff will kill anything from a lion to a buffalo, and there's no antidote. Not even the natives have one. So if Connor has been throwing his weight about, he'd better watch his step; and so had you if it comes to that, should you come in contact with a tribe that has it in for Connor.'

'Thanks,' acknowledged Biggles. 'I see what you mean. How did you get this information?'

'We hear things. We have friends among the Bushmen.'

'Well, I won't pretend to be interested in Connor's behaviour,' Biggles said frankly. 'That's your affair. I want to talk to Browning.'

'Why not wait here? Connor has a jeep. From time to time he has to come into town for stores. One thing's certain. He – and this goes for Browning if he's with him – can't live on what he finds in the Kalahari. Only a Bushman can do that, and it takes *him* all his time.'

'He may not show up here for some while, and we haven't all that time to spare. The jeep, like Browning's plane, should be easy to spot from the air.'

'If you see the plane on the ground, what will you do? Land?'

'Probably, if the ground is suitable. It should be. After all, as a pilot, Browning wouldn't be such a fool as to land where there's a risk of bending his undercart; of not being able to take off again.'

The policeman nodded. 'That's true. What exactly do you intend to do with Browning if you do catch up with him?'

'For the time being, as I've said, merely ask him a few questions. He could tell us what we want to know.'

'If he's back with Connor, as seems likely, we, too, would like to know what they're up to. Regulations are tight on the buying and selling of diamonds. If you should see anything suspicious you might let us know. On the other hand, if we can help you in any way, just say the word.'

'I'll certainly do that,' agreed Biggles. 'I take it you have no aircraft for your own use?'

'Normally, with road, rail and air links with important places, we don't need a private plane.'

'By the way, what's your name if I should want to get in touch with you?'

'Carter. Bill Carter. You can contact me at police headquarters.'

'Okay.'

The policeman went on his way.

As Biggles and Bertie made for the airport, Bertie said: 'Nice lad, that. He didn't like to say too much, but it's pretty clear this chap Connor is a bit of a tough character.'

'It begins to look like that. He's not an uncommon type here, I imagine. No doubt that's why the police are armed.'

Half an hour later the *Merlin* was in the air, climbing as it headed east over country that was at first under cultivation, but soon became more open and arid. Roads, tracks and an occasional settlement became farther apart and finally fizzled out, leaving only an apparently endless expanse of barren earth with occasional scrub that might be described as semi-desert.

'So this is the Kalahari – or the fringe of it,' Biggles observed. 'The sort of country I dislike flying over more than most. I get the willies, imagining I hear one of the engines running rough.'

'Same as you, old boy,' returned Bertie warmly.

'Well, at least we knew what it was like before we came here,' said Biggles philosophically. 'Keep your eyes on the ground for any signs of what we're looking for. I'll watch the air, in case Browning is doing a spot of aviation. Tell me if you spot any big game. It might be a guide if Browning and Connor are still seriously concerned with the skins of dead animals for ladies to drape round themselves, like people did thousands of years ago when they'd nothing else to keep out the cold.'

Biggles settled the *Merlin* for level flight at a thousand feet, high enough to give a wide view, yet low enough, in the good visibility, for details on the ground to be seen and identified. Having no particular objective, he flew by compass to keep track of his position. There were in fact practically no definite, possible objectives; the largest scale map he had been able to procure before he left England offered only a blank white space with even conventional signs few and far between.

For some time there was no sign of life of any sort.

Nothing at all. No movement anywhere to relieve the monotony of the scene. Not even a smudge of smoke to indicate the presence of human beings, perhaps an odd party of Bushmen. As Bertie observed, the whole place looked dead, and 'as flat as a bally pancake.'

However, it turned out he was speaking too soon, as the appearance of a straggling group of ostriches was soon to testify. They took no notice of the aircraft. After that, a certain amount of game was seen, in particular in the region of some sparse, parched-looking scrub; but there was nothing to be compared with the more fertile parts of the continent. Zebra and wildebeeste were the most common animals, although even these did not occur in large herds. Once a party of deer or antelope, gemsbok Biggles thought, stared up at the aircraft. If there were any big 'cats' they were not in evidence. Bertie pointed out what he took to be a lion, but on closer investigation it turned out to be a hyena. A solitary jackal skulked near a heap of sun-bleached bones. Considering the area of ground covered by the plane, it was, they agreed, a thin population.

'All I can say, old boy, is this,' declared Bertie. 'If Connor and Browning are hoping to get rich on leopard skins they'll have to put in a lot of overtime. What beats me is, why Browning, if he has a pocketful of rubies, should come back to a dreary place like this. I could think of more salubrious spots.'

'In the more salubrious spots, as you call 'em, there are likely to be more police. Maybe that's the answer. There is this about the Kalahari. For a criminal on the run, it should at least be safe. No doubt there are more flourishing areas here than we have seen; I didn't expect to cover twenty-five thousand square miles in one day. Animals will be within reach of water. They must know where to get a drink, otherwise they'd die. Where there is most wild life one would expect to find the Bushmen. They have to eat, too. The same

with Connor, and Browning if he is with him. I don't thin
we can judge the place by what we have seen so far. I'r
content for the moment to have a look at it. Later on we ca
go farther afield, farther from the fringe of civilization.
wouldn't expect to find Connor, or anyone else in his righ
mind, in this part of the desert. But we shall find ther
eventually. I still maintain that anyone would be clever t
hide a plane, or a jeep, in this sort of country. A jeep can'
move without leaving tracks. Had there been any we shoul
have seen them. On open ground like this they'd show u
like railway lines – anyway, until there was enough wind t
blow dust over them.'

So saying, Biggles began a long slow turn to the nortl
with the object of taking in new ground on the retur
journey. 'We've done about two hundred miles,' he went or
after a glance at the watch on the instrument panel. 'We'v
still a lot of ground to cover, by the time we get back w
shall have done enough for today.'

The plane droned on under a flat blue sky, bumping
little in the unstable, superheated atmosphere.

'Don't they ever get rain here?' asked Bertie, lookin
down at the tired, parched landscape.

'According to the book, at certain times of the year the
can get some pretty fierce thunderstorms,' replied Biggles
'Obviously they must get rain sometimes, or the whol
country would die completely.'

To record the return journey to base would be mere repeti
tion. It is sufficient to say that nothing whatever was seen t
excite their interest or curiosity. Bertie studied the ground
Biggles watched above and around; but if Browning's *Mar
tin* was in the air, it could not have been in their part of th
sky, for nothing was seen of it.

They returned to the aerodrome without incident, with
out trouble, a little tired but not disappointed. As Biggle
remarked, it was early days yet to give up hope.

They found one item of information waiting for them. It came from Bill Carter, the policeman. He had been in touch with all the airports within reach of Windhoek, Keetmanshoop and Upington to the south, and even as far as Mafeking, Mahalapye and Johannesburg to the east, but there was no record of Browning having landed at any one of them.

'Unless he had a breakdown somewhere, it looks more than ever he's on the carpet somewhere in the Kalahari,' commented Biggles.

CHAPTER 8

A SHOT – FROM WHERE?

BIGGLES was getting worried. He did not say much, but Bertie knew it. For three days the *Merlin* had been in the air, covering long distances on a definite plan to avoid going over the same ground twice, even as far east as Bechuanaland, all this without any sign or hint of what they were seeking. Bertie reckoned they had covered at least two thirds of the desert. It was disappointing. They had not expected to be away from home for as long as this. Any day there might be a signal from the Air Commodore recalling them, and it was provoking to have to leave a task unfinished.

There had been pockets where a fair amount of wild life, both animals and birds, had collected, perhaps indicating a dried up spring or water-hole, although no actual water had been seen. These had been investigated from a low level in the assumption that Connor was most likely to be found where there was most game; but in the end the result had always been the same. They had seen one or two small parties of natives. Biggles had been tempted to land, thinking they might know something, but had refrained for two reasons. In the first place the ground had always been rough, which would have been dangerous, and secondly, unable to speak the Bushman language, it would probably have been a useless effort, anyway.

'I'm beginning to think we're wasting our time,' Biggles said wearily, at the end of the second blank day.

'I couldn't agree more,' returned Bertie. 'They're not

here; or if they are they've found a place to tuck themselves well out of sight. They can't be moving about, or surely we'd have seen fresh tracks of the jeep on the ground. I can't imagine Browning using his plane. No man in his right mind would go hopping about in an aircraft over this sort of ground.'

They had spoken to Bill Carter at the police station. He had no suggestion to make. No word had come in of any unusual happenings in the desert. The natives knew all about aeroplanes, of course. If they had seen one they would hardly bother to report it. To them one plane was like another. Had they seen one it was most likely to have been the *Merlin*.

Carter had asked if they had seen the Etosha Pan yet? It was the most outstanding feature in the Kalahari. They couldn't mistake it. Game was always there, although at this time of the year it was mostly a sea of mud, and would remain like that until the next rain.

Biggles said no, pointing out they had started at the southern end of the desert and were working their way north towards it.

'Do you think Connor might be there?' Biggles queried.

'He might be, but it's not very likely.'

'Why not, if there's plenty of game there?'

'That's where he'd be most likely to bump into Joe Villiers.'

'Who's he?'

'He acts as something between a game warden and a native Commissioner. We don't see him very often.' Carter grinned. 'He's one of these queer people who seem to love deserts.'

'Is there any chance that either Connor or Browning may have slipped into town while we were out?'

'Very unlikely. Connor would have made for the nearest

pub and we should have heard about it. Had you any reason for thinking they might have been in?'

'I thought Browning might have come in to post a letter – that is, assuming there's no other post-office within reach. We're pretty sure he posted one letter from here, to a girl in England. That was one of our clues to his probable whereabouts. He might continue to write to keep in touch with the lady. He certainly made for here when he left England. There's no doubt about that. He left a trail down Africa as wide open as a motorway. That has always struck me as a bit queer.'

'What else could he have done when he needed petrol?'

'He could have used a false name.'

'That would have meant having false papers.'

'That sort of thing has been done.'

'What about his passport? He couldn't travel without one. Unless Browning was a regular crook, and knew one of these underworld types who forge passports, he'd have a job to get a fake.'

'I suppose so.' Biggles hesitated. 'I've never thought about it. I've always taken it for granted that being British he would travel under a British passport. Perhaps I should have checked that at the head passport office in London, but it never occurred to me. I wonder if they have a record of his passport at the airport. I'll speak to them about it.'

'If you like, to save you time and trouble, I could ring them from here.'

'Thanks.'

Carter put through the call and asked the question. There was some delay while a check was made. Finally he got his answer and hung up. Looking at Biggles, he said: 'You'll be interested to know that Browning wasn't travelling on a British passport. He had a passport issued in South Africa. That sounds as if he might be a South African. Went to England from South Africa in the first place.'

Biggles, whose eyes had opened wide as he listened, shook his head sadly. 'Which all goes to show people in our line of business should never take anything for granted. I've been careless. It now looks as if when he landed here he was actually on his way home.'

'We can all make mistakes,' consoled Carter. He went on: 'Has it struck you that Browning deliberately left a wide open trail? He not only knew he'd be followed. He *wanted to be followed*.'

'Why should he?'

'To lead the police up the garden path. It sounds to me as if he dragged a red herring to give you a nice easy scent to follow, to take you away from a confederate who was in the business with him. He was prepared for you to follow him as far as this – but no farther. Now he's playing hard to find. He's lying low. Very low. I fancy you're going to have all your work cut out to find this wily bird.'

'You're right,' Biggles answered with a touch of chagrin. 'This South African passport, and what you've just said, puts a fresh complexion on the whole affair. Thanks. But we'll catch up with him. We haven't finished yet. This trail is bound to end somewhere, and wherever that may be we shall eventually arrive at it.'

That was the end of the conversation with Carter.

When they were outside Bertie said: 'I don't want to rub it in, old boy, but it seems to me that Bill Carter can teach us something.'

'On this occasion, anyway,' agreed Biggles. 'There's a lot in what he says about the possibility of Browning leading us up a gum tree to protect someone else. I started off on the wrong foot, maybe because it all looked easy. Then, having got into the wood, we couldn't see it for trees.'

'But who could Browning be trying to protect?'

'I can think of only one person. Lady Caroline.'

'But that doesn't make sense. Why should she rob her own

father of something that will come to her, anyway, when he dies?'

'If we knew that we should know the lot,' replied Biggles. 'It was obvious from the beginning that that young lady knew plenty. That was why she wouldn't talk. Nothing would make her. No matter. We shall have to manage without her. It's just a matter of time. Let's get on with it. I'm more determined than ever to get to the bottom of this little conundrum.'

It was on the fourth day that the situation changed.

The reconnaissance started in the usual way; a direct flight out, north of the route previously taken, then a long wide turn to the left to bring the plane back to its base over fresh ground. It happened on the way home. Bertie, who as usual was watching below, suddenly cried out: 'Here, hold on a minute, chaps, what the deuce is that down there?'

Biggles tilted the machine in a gentle turn, the better to get a clear picture in the direction in which Bertie's eyes were staring. For some seconds he did not speak. Then he said, slowly: 'I don't understand this. What do you make of it?'

'Looks like buildings of some sort. A village, or something like it, that has been well and truly blitzed.'

'According to my information, there's nothing like that here,' declared Biggles. 'There's nothing shown on the map. Surely had there been anything here we'd have been told about it. Carter would have mentioned it. It can't be anything to do with the local natives; they don't build houses. Let's have a closer look.'

So saying, Biggles cut the engines and went down in a steep sideslip, to lose height quickly to about a hundred feet. Having brought the machine to even keel, he circled slowly over the objects that had attracted Bertie's attention. Presently he said: 'There's no doubt about it. They're ruins of some sort. Not that there's much left of 'em. How extraordinary.'

'Do you feel like going down to have a look?'

'Not me. I'm not taking any chances without a better reason than curiosity. What's the point of it? There's nobody here, no plane, no jeep, or we'd be bound to see 'em. We'll ask Carter about this when we get back.'

Biggles climbed back to his usual altitude and continued on his course. It was more comfortable flying at a thousand feet than close to the ground where heat waves made the air choppy. They kept a sharp lookout, but saw no signs of life. Interest waned as they left the ruins behind them.

About a quarter of an hour later, in which time they had covered some fifty or sixty miles, Bertie again called Biggles' attention to something on the ground. He was at that moment watching the sky.

They were now passing over an area where, possibly because there were some wide, straggling groups of scrub, there was a fair amount of game, more than they had seen so far in one place; almost certain proof, Biggles had remarked, of water no great distance away.

'What the devil is all that?' exclaimed Bertie. 'Looks like a bally castle, or an old temple, or something of that sort.'

Again Biggles concentrated his attention. There was no mistaking the object of Bertie's interest. Not only was it a building, gaunt and stark, standing four square to the winds of heaven, but it was of considerable size, covering not much less than an acre of ground.

'What about that, eh?' queried Bertie. 'It looks as if we're doing a spot of exploring on the side – if you see what I mean. Put some new marks on the map; tell Carter a few things he didn't know.'

'Don't fool yourself,' returned Biggles. 'He must know all about this. It couldn't have been overlooked. It stands out of this flat landscape like a windmill in a meadow.' He was doing another circuit from a low level.

'But what can it be? What does it look like to you?'

'It looks to me more than anything like an old fortress. If this was anywhere in Europe I wouldn't think twice about it. In fact, even here I'm pretty sure that's what it was intended to be, although who would build a fort in a place like this, and for what possible purpose, I wouldn't try to guess. Look at the size of it. That surrounding wall must be a quarter of a mile long. And those outbuildings. There must be enough accommodation to house the entire population of the Kalahari – from what we've seen of it. Somebody, sometime, must have put in a heck of a lot of work.'

'Did the ancient Egyptians ever come as far south as this? They were great lads for building in a big way – pyramids, and that sort of lark.'

'I'm no authority, but I'd say it's unlikely that the Egyptians ever came this way. There's nothing Egyptian about this lot, anyhow. That building looks comparatively modern.'

'Where did all the rock come from?'

'I'd make a bet it's mostly concrete, or cement blocks. What does it matter? The only thing that concerns us, it's as dead as the rest of this miserable country. There's nobody here, or they'd be out to have a squint at us. Planes can't pass this way so often that anyone below is no longer interested in looking at 'em. There is this about it. Apparently the animals don't like the look of it. You'll notice they're keeping their distance.'

'Is it worth landing to have a close look?'

Biggles studied the ground. 'I suppose we could. The surface doesn't look too bad. But as I said before there doesn't seem much object in it. What could we see from ground level that we can't see from up here? No. It isn't worth taking a thousand to one risk. If anything went wrong it'd be a long and uncomfortable hike home. We'll hear what Carter has to say about it. He must know what it is. Don't ask me to believe that a place this size has so far passed unnoticed even in the Kalahari.'

Biggles resumed his homeward flight.

Five minutes later, as they were cruising over a mixture of scrub and flat-topped trees, there came a sudden whip-like crack from some part of the airframe. In a flash Biggles was testing the controls. He looked at the wing on each side, glanced at the instruments and then turned startled eyes to meet Bertie's. 'What the devil was that?' he rapped out. 'Everything all right your side?'

'Nothing wrong that I can see.' Bertie, too, was looking alarmed.

'What was it?'

'Haven't a clue, old boy.'

'What did it sound like to you?'

'Since you put it like that, had there been a war on I'd have said it was a bullet hitting us somewhere.'

Biggles nodded. 'War or no war, I have a feeling you could be right. That's what it sounded like to me.'

'You really think some idiot had a crack at us?' Bertie looked incredulous.

'What else is there to think?' Biggles said.

'Who would shoot at us, and why? Where could the shot have come from?'

'Never mind where it came from.'

'Press on, in case there are any more where that one came from,' requested Bertie, urgently.

'I think that's the drill,' answered Biggles. 'We'll have a thorough check-up when we get back. If that wasn't a bullet it's time we had a complete overhaul. If there's one thing that has always given me the heeby-jeebies it's the thought of structural failure.'

Nothing more was said. Biggles flew straight home, putting as little strain as possible on the machine. Nothing happened. He breathed more freely as they touched down.

As soon as he had taxied to the usual parking place and

switched off, he jumped down and began a systematic search of all the outer surfaces. Bertie helped, taking the other side of the fuselage.

Presently Biggles called him from the port wing. 'Come and take a look at this.'

Bertie hurried round. Biggles, grim-faced, was pointing to a tiny round hole in the leading edge. 'So now we know,' he said. 'It *was* a bullet. Went right through, of course. No harm done, but it'll need a patch.'

Bertie pursed his lips. 'Well, stiffen the crows!' he breathed. 'So there must have been somebody there.'

'Somebody who took jolly good care we didn't see *him*. He'd hear us coming and took cover. I'll tell you something else. Whoever he is he's a crack shot with a rifle. It takes some doing to hit an aircraft in the air with a single bullet.'

'But why shoot at us? We'd done nothing.'

'Obviously he didn't like the look of us. Maybe he did it to discourage us from going too close. He may even have hoped to bring us down. If that was his idea he defeated his object. I'm going back, and this time I'll try to be a little less conspicuous.'

'But who on earth would do a thing like that?'

Biggles shook his head. 'I don't know, but I'd risk two guesses.'

'Browning?'

'Possibly. But what we know of him wouldn't suggest he might stoop to murder.'

'Connor?'

'That's more likely – but we could still be wrong. What other white men are there in the Kalahari? Bushmen don't carry guns. But instead of standing here guessing, let's have a word with Carter. We'll do that right away.'

CHAPTER 9

CARTER HAS SOME ANSWERS

BIGGLES and Bertie went straight to the police station and may have been lucky to find Carter there, disengaged.

'It's us again,' announced Biggles apologetically. 'Sorry to trouble you, but we're a bit mystified about one or two things we've seen today and thought you might be able to throw some light on them.'

'You mean, in the Kalahari?'

'Yes. We've just done another long reconnaissance.'

'What did you see?'

'The first thing we saw was a town, or the ruins of one. We were more than somewhat surprised because there's nothing shown on the map and we'd been told nothing about it.'

A slow smile spread over Carter's face. 'Ah! So that's it. You spotted the lost city.'

'Lost city! What lost city? A city is a pretty big thing to lose. Who lost it, and when?'

'Nobody knows.'

'You didn't say anything to us about it when we were talking about the Kalahari, and what we might find in it.'

'It's my business to deal with facts and leave the romance to the story-tellers. However, I'll tell you all I know. We needn't stand here. Come into my office and I'll send for a cup of coffee.'

Presently Carter was telling his story. 'This lost city yarn is nothing new,' he began. 'In Africa there have always been

81

tales of lost cities, lost tribes – some of them white – and what have you. This one started years ago when two tough old prospectors named Anderson and Farini tried trekking across the Kalahari by ox-wagon. They weren't interested in cities, lost or otherwise. What they were looking for, of course, was gold, or diamonds, or both. To such men the unknown offers an irresistible lure. They weren't fools. They chose their time after the occasional rainy season when they could reckon on finding some water still in the shallow pans in the desert. They had a pretty bad time and eventually returned without finding what they had been looking for. However, in talking about their trip, they mentioned that out in the desert, near a dried-up river bed, they had come across some ruins. "Like a place after an earthquake," was how Farini described them. Nobody took him seriously.'

'Why not? Was there any reason why the men should concoct such a tale? Had they anything to gain by it?'

'Not that I know of. They weren't archaeologists. They had no interest in ruins and they said so. Farini, apparently annoyed by having his story questioned, said he could prove it. It so happened that he had taken a camera with him so was able to produce photographic evidence of his ruins. But the camera was an old-fashioned one, and the heat may have affected the plates, because what the pictures showed might have been anything. The critics said the so-called ruins were merely a collection of stones and rock worn into queer shapes by wind-blown sand. That, for the time being, was where the story ended. It cropped up again when another explorer, a man named Smith, reported that he had seen the lost city and declared that the ruins were in fact hand-cut stones. There were pavements, and so on. This was enough to send a party of scientists out hot-foot to have a look at the ruins. They couldn't find them. They were certainly not where they were supposed to be. Other expeditions have been out to look for the lost city, but they couldn't find it.'

'Are we to believe that the men who claimed to have seen he ruins were all liars?'

'I've kept an open mind about it,' Carter said. 'The experts have a theory about the place, of course. Experts always have a theory for something they can't explain.'

'What is this theory?' inquired Biggles.

'They say there may be ruins somewhere out there in the desert, but every so often a particularly strong wind buries them under a mass of sand. Then another storm comes along and uncovers them again. And so it goes on. Sometimes the ruins are there, sometimes they aren't. But what are we arguing about now you say you've seen them?'

'They certainly looked like ruins to me, although I wouldn't swear to it,' put in Bertie. 'I was looking down from upstairs.'

'What does it matter?' Biggles said impatiently. 'I'm not interested in ruins. Nor have I any interest in gold or diamonds. I'm looking for something that looks like an aircraft, a jeep, or better still, two white men.'

'So you haven't found 'em yet.'

'Not yet.'

'Nor any sign of 'em?'

'I wouldn't go as far as to say that,' answered Biggles in a curious voice. 'I'll come back to that in a moment. Can you tell us anything about this? On our way home we flew over a building that looked like a castle of some sort. And I can assure you there's no doubt about this. It wasn't an outcrop of rock, or anything like that. We both saw it, as large as life.'

'Well, at least there's no mystery about that,' declared Carter cheerfully. 'You must have seen one of the old forts.'

'Forts! What old forts?'

'You know that this part of Africa used to be a German colony – German South-West Africa.'

'Yes, I knew that,' confirmed Biggles.

'When the Germans first settled here they had a lot of trouble with a warlike tribe of natives called Ovambos. Quite a few of the settlers were murdered by them. British settlers in other parts of Africa had the same trouble you remember. The Zulus, for instance. To deal with this nuisance the Germans had to introduce and maintain a strong military garrison to teach the raiders a lesson. And as the Germans are thorough in anything they do, as we well know, they made a real job of it. In a word, they built forts to keep the Ovambos at a distance. They weren't flimsy stockades, either. They threw up massive fortifications that were impregnable against anything less than artillery. Of course, the Ovambos, what there are left of them, no longer give trouble, and the forts are slowly falling into ruins. I've seen one of them called Namatoni. It encloses a spring. A German cavalry regiment was stationed there. You can still see the stables and troughs where they watered their horses. Some of the old frontier posts carry notices like *Deutches Schutlgebeit*. Relics like empty beer bottles and ration tins still lie about. Whereabouts were you when you saw this fort?'

Biggles described the position.

'That sounds as if it might be Fort Schwarz,' Carter said. 'I've never seen it; I've never been as far out as that; but I imagine it's much like the rest. All these forts were built on the same sort of plan. You won't find anything there, except perhaps the well, or water-hole, and that will probably have silted up.'

'I wouldn't bet too much on that,' said Biggles, dryly.

'Why, did you see something?'

'No. But someone certainly spotted us; someone who apparently hated the sight of us.'

'What do you mean?'

'Someone had a crack at us with a rifle.'

Carter stared. 'The devil he did! Are you sure of this?'

'Quite sure. We heard the impact of the bullet, and it happens that's a sound we've heard before. When we got home we went over the machine and found the hole.'

Carter looked serious. 'That could only have been a white man. I wonder who it could have been!'

'Do you know of anyone in the desert, or this part of it, except Connor and possibly Browning?'

'I know of no one, although of course some hunter may have come in from the east, or perhaps Portuguese territory to the north. Do you know exactly where the bullet came from?'

'I don't think it was actually fired from the fort. We'd left it under our tail and were over what looked like an area of fairly dense scrub.'

'Could it have been an accident?'

Biggles smiled cynically. 'It was a jolly queer one if it was, to hit the only thing in the sky for a hundred miles. I suppose it couldn't have been a Bushman?'

'Not a chance. They don't carry rifles. They still prefer to hunt as they always have, with bows and poisoned arrows. It seems to me that Fort Schwarz would be a good place for you to keep away from.'

'Why keep away from it? There's now some reason to go back to it. We've been looking for something, and this is the first hint we've had that we may have found it.'

'Does that mean you intend to go back there?'

'Of course. What else?'

Carter looked serious. 'Be careful what you get up to. As you know, we've no aircraft, so if you should get in a mess, it's unlikely we'd be able to do anything to help you.'

'I shall watch it,' promised Biggles. 'We shan't take more risks than we're compelled to; but we came here to do a job and we shall press on with it.'

'Okay. I can understand that. Let me know how you get on.'

'I shall do that,' Biggles said.

'When do you think of flying back to Fort Schwarz?'

'Tomorrow.'

'Are you contemplating landing?'

'Yes – if we can find a place to get down.'

'Well, if you don't come back I shall have a rough idea of where to find you,' concluded Carter.

Biggles nodded; and with that they took their departure.

CHAPTER 10

FORT SCHWARZ

THE following morning the *Merlin* was in the air early, Bigles anxious to get the business that had brought them to Africa finished one way or the other as quickly as possible. Apart from sending home a signal to report his safe arrival at Windhoek, having nothing to report he had not been in touch with the office, and he knew that any day now there might come a message from the Air Commodore ordering him to return home. The case being merely of common felony would not be of sufficient importance to keep him from something with a more serious interpretation that might crop up at headquarters. Wherefore he was keen to finish what he had come to do, instead of going home no wiser for a long and arduous journey.

He headed straight for what had become the centre of interest, the abandoned military building which Carter had named Fort Schwarz, now probably in a state of dilapidation. He was prepared to risk a landing if necessary; indeed, he realized it was unlikely he would be able to find out what was going on there unless he did. It was true the bullet that had been fired at them had not come from the actual fort; but the fort was no great distance from the sun-dried forest, so it was reasonable to suppose there might be some connection. He realized too, that the rifle shot might have nothing whatever to do with Browning or Connor; but in view of the improbability of anyone else being in the region, it was a possibility not to be ignored. Just what he would do

if he found the two men, or even one of them, he did no
know. That would depend on the circumstances. What th
men did; how they behaved.

With all this Bertie was in full agreement.

One aspect that puzzled him was the scarcity of game nea
the fort. Why was that? If there was water there, and ther
must have been water at the time of its occupation by th
German garrison, one might have expected more game, no
less. Of course, if the animals had been shot at regularly, by
someone living in the fort, that would account for it. Any
man living in the desert, unless he had a big stock of canned
food, would have to kill game to live.

Another factor was the absence of Bushmen near the old
fort. He knew from what he had read that the natives as a
general rule, being nomadic in habit, huddled together in
primitive bough-shelters; but surely that did not mean they
would not occupy more substantial dwellings, such as the
fort, if they were available – particularly if there was water
there. Or would they? There might be some doubt about
that. At all events, there appeared to be none in or around
the fort. Had they some reason for keeping well clear of
it?

The sun was up, and as usual blazing down from a
cloudless blue sky to torture the arid earth, when the *Merlin*
reached its first objective, which was the tangle of scrub and
mixed dwarf timber, mostly acacia, from which it seemed
that the shot had come. The only living creatures in sight
were a family of ostriches on the fringe. They took fright
and raced away at the near approach of the aircraft. Biggles
circled, at first keeping a fair height, aware that what had
happened the previous day might happen again with more
serious results. But this was a risk that had to be accepted if
they were to accomplish anything.

'See anything?' he asked Bertie.

'Not a bally thing. If there's a plane or a jeep down there it must be jolly well camouflaged, that's all I can say. I suppose that's possible.'

Biggles agreed. 'But why should Connor or Browning go to that trouble when up to yesterday a plane must have been the last thing they'd expect to come this way? We're miles from any regular route. They'd know that. Anyhow, it wouldn't be easy to push any sort of vehicle into those bushes without leaving marks of some sort.'

By this time, still circling and losing height, the machine was down to about a hundred feet. This, it was realized, was asking for trouble should the unknown marksman still be about. Actually, as Bertie suspected, Biggles was deliberately tempting him to try another shot, to reveal his position. This did not happen. Nothing moved.

'Are you going down?' asked Bertie.

'Not here,' decided Biggles. 'There doesn't seem to be any point in it.'

'That stuff is pretty thick in places. It could provide cover for an elephant.'

'We're not looking for elephants. Not that I'd expect to see any here. What could we do if we did go down? Blunder about, scratching ourselves to pieces and building up an almighty thirst? Not for me. We'll go on to the fort. We're more likely to find something there. Anyone taking up residence hereabouts would prefer to live under cover than sleep rough in the open where there's always a chance of a hyena making a grab at your face while you're dreaming. It has happened. If the man who took a shot at us has been living in the fort there are bound to be signs of it.'

While he had been speaking Biggles had straightened out and now flew on towards the fort, the only conspicuous landmark in the flat, open country, apart from a long, shallow gulley that might have been the bed of a river that had either dried up for good or run dry during the present rainless season.

Biggles made his first run straight over the fort which, far from being a ruin as might have been expected, appeared to have stood up well to the weather. This applied to the surrounding defensive wall, which enclosed an area of sandy ground large enough to provide a parade ground for a battalion of infantry or a squadron of cavalry. A wide gap in the wall suggested there had once been entrance gates, the only way to gain admission; but the actual gates, perhaps made of wood, had gone. There was no sign of life. The *Merlin* made a second run, at right angles from the first. Still nothing moved.

'If there's anyone there I'll eat my helmet,' said Bertie.

'If there is anyone about he's had second thoughts about taking pot shots at us, anyhow,' returned Biggles. 'I don't get it. There must have been someone not far away when we came over yesterday. Where's he gone?'

'If it was Connor he could have gone for a run in his jeep.'

'If so I don't think Browning could be with him.'

'Why not?'

'Because as far as I can see there's nowhere down there where he could put his plane. A plane is what I'm looking for. If Browning is in the Kalahari it must be parked somewhere. You can't hide a plane up your sleeve. And you couldn't put one in the fort, even if it had folding wings, that's for sure.'

'How about putting our wheels down and having a look round the place?'

Biggles looked doubtful. 'You realize that once we're on the carpet we shall be vulnerable? I'd hate to get a bullet through the tank in a place like this. However, as we're here we might as well settle the question once and for all.'

Biggles made several runs outside the wall, on the side where the entrance gates had been, studying the ground intently. There was very little in the way of obstructions; a stunted bush or two, and a few stones, but nothing to make a landing risky, much less dangerous. The surface of the ground looked hard; more like firm, well-packed gravel than soft sand. Apparently satisfied, Biggles took a long approach run and gliding in made a normal landing, running to a stop close to the gap in the wall. Leaving the engines ticking over, he did not move. His eyes were on the entrance.

'Sit still,' he said tersely. 'We'll give anyone time enough, just in case there's anyone here, to show himself. Unless he's deaf he must have heard us arrive.'

They waited, Biggles with a hand on the throttle ready for a quick take-off should it become necessary. After two or three minutes he switched off. 'Okay,' he said, as the engines died. 'Stay where you are till I'm on my feet.' He jumped down. Again he waited, his eyes on the gap in the wall. No one appeared. 'Right,' he told Bertie. 'There can't be anyone here. You can get out.'

'Aren't you going to take the machine inside?' asked Bertie, as he got out.

'I hadn't thought of it,' replied Biggles. 'If we leave it where it is we should be able to get off in a hurry if that became necessary.'

'We would look silly if while we were inside someone came along and made a dent in it.'

'You could be right,' conceded Biggles. 'Come to think of it, it might be as well to have the machine where we can keep an eye on it. The yard looks as dead as a cemetery, but anything could happen in a place like this. We'd better be on the safe side and take her in. But is the gateway wide enough to go through without scraping wings?'

'I think so. Anyhow we can test it.'

As they strode to the opening, Biggles said: 'I'll tell you this. We'd be wasting our time looking for tracks. The surface is as hard as concrete and a plane would ride over it without leaving a mark. So would a jeep if it comes to that. As you can see we've hardly scratched it.'

'The tyres of a jeep are narrower than ours,' Bertie pointed out.

'Maybe, but unless Connor is a fool he'd keep his tyres pretty slack in this heat to allow for expansion.' Biggles paced the width of the entrance. 'Good. She'll just go through,' he announced. 'You stand here and guide me in. I'll go and fetch her.' He walked back to the *Merlin* leaving Bertie standing in the middle of the entrance.

With Bertie signalling with his hands, the aircraft was manoeuvred into the compound without any difficulty, the wing tips having a clearance of a foot on each side. Biggles taxied on a short distance, turned to face the exit, switched off and got down. 'Okay,' he said. 'There's obviously nobody here, or they'd have been out before this.'

Together they surveyed the scene. Not that there was much to look at. The main building, the actual fort, was long and squat, consisting only of two storeys, which made it look out of proportion. The roof was flat. All round it ran a low crenellated wall, giving the place the appearance of a medieval castle. Apparently as a last resort it could be defended from the roof. It looked grey, grim and menacing, as forts usually do. It presented a blank face to the world except for the single door, which stood open, and two rows of windows. These were unglazed but protected with horizontal bars. On the ground floor a few bars had been wrenched off.

'Bushmen may have been responsible for that,' Biggles said. 'No doubt the iron would be useful to them for knives, arrow heads and the like.' He smiled. 'Trust the Boche to take no chances. Only troops with artillery support could hope to take this place. Natives wouldn't have a chance.'

They turned their attention to the compound, or enclosure, which had probably been used as a parade ground. It was of some considerable size. All along the inside of one wall was a continuous row of buildings that may have been store rooms or possibly stables, since in front of them was a drinking trough with a rusty iron pump at one end. They walked over to it. It was empty and dry. Some of the buildings had doors. Others were open to the compound. Biggles remarked that they might just be wide enough to take a jeep, but certainly not a plane, however small.

Looking along the open ground, his eyes came to rest on a black patch at the far end against the wall. 'What's all that?' he said.

'Looks as though there's been a fire; place where the troops burnt their rubbish, perhaps.'

'If that's the answer they didn't go to much trouble about it. Let's have a look.'

As they walked on towards the spot, just before they reached it, against the walls, Biggles paused to glance at a heap of stones, or rather, lumps of old masonry that had been thrown down in a pile. 'That hasn't been there very long,' he observed pensively.

They walked on, their steps quickening as they continued on to where there had obviously been a fire of some size. Even before they reached it the problem had solved itself beyond any possibility of a mistake. They came to a stop, staring at the remains of a burnt-out aircraft, only the metal parts intact; conspicuously, two aero engines and a tangle of wires.

Biggles looked at Bertie with wide-open eyes. Bertie looked at Biggles. For a moment neither of them spoke. Then Biggles drew a deep breath. 'Great grief!' he murmured. 'How the devil did this happen?'

'Browning's *Martin*,' was all Bertie could find to say.

'What else could it be? Twin engines. Wood and fabric construction. It'd burn like a torch.' Biggles took from his pocket a packet of cigarettes and lit one. 'So we've found it,'

he said softly. 'I thought I was past being surprised, but this
is something I did *not* expect.'

'How on earth could it have happened?'

'I can't imagine – unless he was blind drunk.'

'He must have gone flat out smack into the wall.'

Biggles did not answer.

Bertie went on, 'He must have parked the machine in
here. He thought he had room to fly out, but he hadn't.'

Biggles went on into the charred remains. 'I'm not sure
that I agree with you, although I must admit that's how it
looks. He couldn't have been knocked out in the crash. At
all events he must have managed to get clear before the fire
started, otherwise what's left of him would still be here –
unless, of course, somebody got the body out and buried
it.'

'Connor might have done that.'

'I can't think of anyone else who would have been here.
Even if he saw it happen, without any fire-fighting appli-
ances he wouldn't be able to do anything about it. Naturally,
he'd bury the body after the fire had died down. No white
man would just leave it in the plane to rot. Even so, it all
strikes me as a very queer business. *Somebody* must have
removed the body. Let's say it was Connor. He's got a jeep.
One would think the first thing he'd do would be to run into
Windhoek and report what had happened.'

'If Browning's dead we're wasting our time, old boy,' Bertie said practically. 'Dead men can't talk, so we're never
likely to know what he did with the rubies. We might as well
go home.'

'I'd like to have proof that Browning is dead before jump-
ing to conclusions. If we could find Connor he might be able
to tell us what happened here. Whether or not he was here at
the time of the accident, he must know *something* – except
in the unlikely event of Browning being here by himself
without Connor knowing about it.'

Bertie went on, 'I suppose there is just a chance that Browning wasn't too badly injured in the crash and managed to scramble out before the fire really got hold.'

'In that case, where is he?'

'He may have made for Windhoek.'

'In that case, surely we must have seen him. No, that won't do. The trouble is, we haven't a clue as to when this happened.' Biggles threw his cigarette end on the ground and put a foot on it. 'Let's have a look round,' he said shortly, and walked towards the nearest of the out-buildings that lined the inside of the outer wall. Again in passing he paused to look at the rectangular heap of old masonry that had attracted his attention on their way to the burnt-out plane.

'Does that remind you of anything?' he asked.

'Yes.'

'What?'

'A pile of old rubble.'

Biggles frowned. 'This isn't the time to be funny. I mean the shape.'

Bertie shook his head. 'Sorry, old boy. No. Does it remind you of something?'

'Yes.'

'What?'

'Never mind. Work it out for yourself.' Biggles walked on.

They came to the nearest of the outbuildings and looked inside. The doorless entrance let in plenty of light. Biggles pointed to a hayrack above a manger. 'So they were stables,' he said. 'Nothing here.' He walked on to the next doorway. 'Nothing here, either.'

'Are you looking for something?' inquired Bertie curiously.

Biggles had passed on to the next doorway. 'I thought we might find something like that.' He pointed to a pick and shovel resting against the wall. Offering no further explanation, he walked on again towards the next doorway. He came to a sudden stop, looking hard at an object just outside. To all appearances it was an ordinary shallow metal basin.

'You realize what that is?'

Bertie thought for a moment. 'I've never handled one, but isn't it the sort of thing prospectors use for panning gold and diamonds?'

'Yes. Look again.'

'It still looks the same.'

'Doesn't anything odd strike you?'

'Not particularly. I'm only surprised some native hasn't pinched a useful thing like that.'

'There's water in it. There's been no rain. Under this blazing sun water would evaporate in an hour or two. Doesn't *that* strike you as odd?'

'Absolutely, now you mention it. Someone must have filled it – recently. Like putting out a saucer of milk for the cat – if you see what I mean.'

Biggles sniffed. 'You're too right,' he said crisply. 'And I fancy I can smell the cat.' He began to back away.

Bertie pointed to a ring in the wall just outside the doorway. To it was attached a short length of chain. 'Look! It's moving, or am I –' That was as far as he got. He jumped away as from the interior of the stable came a low growl.

It was followed instantly by the creature responsible for it, teeth bared and fur bristling.

It was a leopard.

CHAPTER 11

MICK CONNOR

IT would be hard to say which of them moved the faster,
Biggles or Bertie. Neither had ever moved faster. Each
dashed in a different direction, Biggles feeling in a pocket
for his automatic, admittedly not a very servicable weapon
to use against a wild animal. It was the rattle of a chain that
brought him round. He stopped, seeing the beast had
stopped. It could come no farther, having reached the limit
of its tether, to which it was fastened by a collar round its
neck.

The leopard lay on its stomach, tail flicking, lips drawn
back to show two beautiful sets of teeth. Its eyes glowed
with hate.

Biggles looked at Bertie. Bertie looked at Biggles, a
sheepish smile on his face. 'Someone must be starting a zoo,
or else has a queer taste in pets,' he remarked.

For a moment or two Biggles did not answer. He looked
round the parade ground. He looked at the main building.
He looked at the leopard, still bristling, quivering either
with fear or rage. Then he looked back at Bertie. 'It's only a
cub,' he said.

'A foul-tempered little devil, anyway. I'm keeping out of
reach of those claws. I only hope that bally chain is se-
cure.'

'I'm not thinking of stroking it myself, although I have a
feeling the brute is more afraid of us than we are of it,'
Biggles said. Advancing, he raised an arm sharply, where-

upon the leopard bolted back into its kennel. 'See that?' he went on. 'It's my guess the wretched creature has had some rough treatment. I don't think we have anything to be afraid of as long as we don't interfere with it. Let's consider what this means. Someone must be using this place; come here pretty often, too, to feed and water this unfortunate little beast. The question is, who?'

'Must be a nasty piece of work to keep an animal chained up in a climate like this, that's all I can say,' growled Bertie. 'I feel inclined to let it go.'

'Are you crazy?' retorted Biggles. 'My sympathy doesn't go as far as that. Those teeth and claws would make a pretty mess of your hands and face if you tried to touch it. I can think of a less dangerous idea.'

'I'm listening.'

'I feel like having a look at what's under that heap of stones and bricks we saw nearer the crash.'

'Why should anything be under them?'

'Because someone went to a lot of trouble to put them there. No one except a raving lunatic would play games like that in a place like this just for the hell of it. Since I first saw that pile I had a feeling there was something under it.'

'What do you expect to find?'

'I've got an open mind about it. It could be a parcel of rubies, but I think from the way the stones have been placed it's more likely to be a body. The thing looks to me like a grave.'

'A body! Here, I say, old boy.' Bertie looked shocked. 'Are you thinking of Browning?'

'Why not? We have every reason to think he's dead. Killed in the crash. There aren't so many people in the Kalahari, not around here, anyway. We know of two. One of them must be alive, or the leopard's water bowl would have dried out.'

'But why the stones – to mark the grave?'

'More likely to defeat the hyenas. In this sort of country you can't just put a body in the ground without hyenas smelling it out and digging it up. You have to pile rocks on a grave, and not just for a monument.'

'I say! That's a nasty thought. So you really think there might be a body there?'

'I do.'

'What are you going to do about it?'

'I'm going to see if I'm right; and if I am, who it is. There's a prospector's pick and spade in that stable, possibly the tools that were used to dig the grave, if that's what it is. They've been used recently. As you remarked just now, if Browning is dead we're wasting our time hoping he'll tell us what he did with the rubies, so we might as well go home. Let's see if we can settle the matter here and now.'

'You believe Browning was killed in the crash and Connor buried him?'

'Let's say that's one way of looking at it. If Browning was in fact killed in the crash somebody must have disposed of the body. If it wasn't Connor there must be a third party in the case, although I can't imagine who it could be. If Browning's body isn't here, where is it?'

'Instead of digging for bodies, wouldn't it be easier to find Connor and ask him what he knows?'

'How are we going to find him?'

'Surely all we have to do is wait here; wait for him to come back to feed his beastly little pet.'

'He may not come back.'

'Why not? He couldn't leave an animal to starve to death.'

'He might, if it suited him. From what we've been told, he's spent most of his life shooting big cats, so why need he worry about an odd leopard? Another thought has occurred to me. We believe Browning came here carrying a fortune in rubies. Suppose he told Connor? Or suppose Connor saw them?'

'I see what you mean. You think Connor may have thought it worth while to do a spot of murder to get the jewellery.'

'There's another point. If the rubies were hidden in the plane we're wasting our time looking for them. In the heat of that blaze they'd be reduced to dust – unless, of course someone removed them before setting fire to the plane.'

'You think Connor might have done that?'

'If Connor was after the rubies he wouldn't have been such a fool as to burn the plane, knowing they might be in it. Of course, he might have removed them first. If so, why burn the plane?'

'To get rid of it. If he's the villain he's taken care to make the crash look like an accident.'

'A bit too much like an accident to my way of thinking. find it hard to believe that if Browning was a good enough pilot to fly all the way out here without a crack-up, he'd be daft enough to run into a wall. The man who taught him to fly said he was a first-class pilot. A crash like this doesn't, to me, line up with the work of a good pilot. There's something here that doesn't fit. We're still short of a bit of the jigsaw puzzle. But we could stand here and think of possibilitie for the rest of the day. Let's get cracking and try to find the missing piece. Connor might roll up here any time. Let's get the tools. From what we've been told of Connor, it'd be better if he didn't find us digging. We'd be hard put to find a reasonable excuse.'

Biggles started walking briskly towards the stable where they had seen the pick and spade.

'Just a tick, old boy,' Bertie said sharply. 'Can I hear something?'.

Biggles listened for a moment. 'You can. It's a vehicle of some sort. It sounds to me mighty like a jeep. I have a

eeling that it was a good thing we brought the plane inside.
'd hate to go out and find someone had knocked a hole in
he main tank.'

The vehicle could now be heard more distinctly. It was
approaching and travelling fast.

'What are we going to do?' asked Bertie.

'Do? Nothing. As far as I can see there's nothing we can
do, even if we felt like doing anything – which I don't. This
may be what we've been looking for.'

'What?'

'Connor. Take it easy. Let him do the talking for a start. I
imagine he'll have some questions to ask when he finds us
here.'

A minute later the jeep swung in through the gateway at a
speed which made it evident that the driver did not expect
to find an obstacle in his path. He had to swerve wildly to
avoid the plane, giving the spectators an anxious moment.
Another indication of the driver's reactions was the way he
jammed on his brakes and brought the car to a skidding
stop. For nearly half a minute he sat still, evidently considering the situation. He appeared to be alone. At all events
there was no one else sharing the front seat.

Biggles stood still, watching. So did Bertie. 'Browning
isn't with him, unless he's in the back,' said Biggles. This
was possible because the rear half of the vehicle was fitted
with a sand-coloured canvas hood, probably for protection
against the sun.

The driver got out, revealing his whole body. He was an
enormous man, well over six feet in height. 'It must be Connor,' murmured Biggles. 'There can't be two men as tall as
that in this part of the world. No one else would be likely to
have a jeep, anyway.'

Connor went round to the rear of the vehicle and dragged
something out. It was a small deer or antelope. He let it fall,
and left it as it lay. Then he walked round to the front, clear

of the car. This brought him into full view and it could b
seen that he carried a rifle. He also had another piece o
equipment, hanging from his belt, although until he release
it, it was not easy to see what it was. It turned out to be
short, thick-handled whip, the type known in Africa as
sjambok, made of rhinoceros hide.

'I wonder why he needs that,' conjectured Bertie.

He was soon to see one purpose for it.

It so happened that the leopard cub had emerged from it
retreat and sat basking in the sun outside like the cat it was
Connor shouted something and raised his whip. The anima
did not wait for the lash to fall. It bolted back into th
darkness of its lair.

'The poor brute has had a taste of that whip before to
day,' remarked Biggles softly.

'Then that's all I want to know about Connor,' returne
Bertie in a hard voice. 'A man who'll flog a chained anima
is capable of anything. I'll give him a piece of my min
when –'

'I wouldn't do anything like that,' broke in Biggles. '
have a hunch we may come to blows soon enough. Here h
comes.'

Connor – there could be no doubt about the identity o
the man now walking towards them with the long pur
poseful stride of a man who fears nobody or anything. H
made a fine figure and must have been handsome before a
ugly scar had upset the balance of his face, tanned nearly t
the colour of mahogany by the desert sun. He wore no hat
Apparently he considered a mop of curly black hair, whicl
grew low down on his forehead, sufficient protection. Bushy
eyebrows made a straight line across the top of his nose. On
might have guessed his age at anything between forty an
fifty and still be wrong. He wore little in the way of clothes
An open-necked khaki shirt tucked into soiled drill trousers
clipped at the waist by a cartridge belt, was all, apart from

an old pair of rope-soled canvas shoes. All in all he was a fine specimen of the human race, and would obviously be a redoubtable adversary in any sort of physical combat. He looked ideally suited for the rough, dangerous life he led.

'Who are you?' he demanded, as he came up and stopped. It was a natural question.

'The name's Bigglesworth,' informed Biggles.

Clearly the name meant nothing to the man who had asked the question. 'What the hell are you doing here?' Connor had still not lost all trace of an Irish accent.

Biggles smiled disarmingly. 'I might ask you that.'

'You don't look like tourists.'

'We're not.'

'Prospectors?'

'No.'

'Surveyors, perhaps?'

'No.'

'Well, whoever you are you might be more careful where you park that damned plane of yours. I might have damaged my car.'

'At the rate you were going you would have been more likely to damage my plane.'

Connor scowled. 'How the hell was I to know it was here?'

'True enough,' conceded Biggles. 'On the other hand, I wasn't expecting anyone to arrive in a car. But let's not argue about that. Am I right in thinking you're Mr Connor?'

'You are. What about it?'

'I was hoping to meet you. I thought you might be able to help me. I'm looking for a man named Browning. He flew out into the Kalahari some time ago and hasn't been seen since.'

'Why do you think I should be able to help you?'

'I was given to understand he was a friend of yours.'

'Who told you that?'

'The police in Windhoek. I thought he might have joined you.'

'If you'll believe the police you'll believe anything,' sneered Connor, making it clear how he felt about officials.

'It happens we're police officers ourselves, from England,' Biggles said evenly. 'So you haven't seen Browning?'

'I don't even know the man; and if I did I wouldn't want any truck with him. I work on my own.'

'I see,' murmured Biggles. 'The police must have been misinformed. So you can't help me?'

'No. You'll have to look somewhere else.'

'Any suggestions?'

'No'.

'How often do you come here?'

'What's that got to do with it?'

'It could be important.'

'How?'

'Well, if Browning came here you'd know about it.'

'I come pretty often. He hasn't been here. I look in to feed my leopard. You must have seen it.'

Bertie spoke. 'What's the idea of keeping a leopard on a chain?'

'I'm waiting for it to grow up when its skin will be worth more than it is now. I shot its mother. The cub was too small to have any value. It'll grow.'

'And then you'll kill it?'

'Sure I'll kill it. Leopards are my business. What the hell did you think I was keeping it for?'

'I thought maybe for a pet.'

Connor looked at Bertie incredulously. 'A *pet*,' he echoed, as if he couldn't believe his ears. 'Are you English?'

'I am.'

'Ah! That must account for it.'

'Account for what?'

'This talk about pets. Don't you ever think of nothing else?'

Biggles, feeling the conversation was taking a dangerous turn, broke in. 'Never mind about the leopard. Are you sure Browning hasn't been here?'

'That's what I said, isn't it? Are you calling me a liar?'

'I'm not calling you anything, Mr Connor,' answered Biggles smoothly. 'You say you frequently come here, yet you didn't know Browning had been here. Naturally, that struck me as a little strange.'

'Why should it?'

'Because Browning certainly has been here and I can't understand why you didn't see him.'

'What makes you so darn sure Browning came here?'

'Because the burnt-out wreckage of his plane is up there against the wall.' Biggles pointed.

'Is it? You sure about that?'

'Quite sure.'

'Funny I didn't notice it. All I can say is he must have called when I was away. I'm sometimes away, hunting, for days at a time. There isn't as much game about here as there used to be.'

'Does anyone else ever come here?'

'Not that I know of.'

'I'm wondering what could have happened to Browning. If he wasn't killed in the crash he must have been hurt. His body isn't in the wreck. Dead or alive, someone must have moved him.'

'Begorra, you have been busy,' scoffed Connor. 'It wasn't me. I've something better to do than clutter myself up with bodies, dead or alive. Mebbe this feller Browning started walking to Windhoek.'

Biggles nodded. 'That may be the answer. At any rate, you know nothing about him?'

'Not a thing. How many times do you want telling?'

'That's enough, I think. Very well, Mr Connor, since you say you can't help us, I needn't waste any more of your time. We might as well move on.'

Connor betrayed himself somewhat by looking relieved. 'That suits me,' he said. 'I'm a busy man.'

'I'm sure you are.'

'Where are you going now?'

'I haven't decided yet. Probably back to Windhoek. Come on, Bertie.' Biggles started walking towards the plane.

Bertie kept close to him. 'Are you letting him get away with this cock-and-bull story?'

'What else can we do? We shan't get anywhere by arguing with him and I've no intention of starting a punch-up in which we'd certainly get the worst of it.'

'He's a liar.'

'Of course he is, and a fluent one. That sticks out a mile. But if he won't tell the truth we can't make him. It's better to let him think we're a daft pair of Englishmen who can be fooled into believing anything. You can go and guide me through the gateway.' Biggles began to climb into the machine.

'Just a minute, old boy.' Bertie looked round to make sure they were well out of earshot. 'There's something you should know.'

Biggles lifted an eyebrow.

'There's somebody in the fort,' whispered Bertie.

'How do you know?'

'I saw a face looking through the bars of one of the upper windows.'

'What sort of face?'

'A white face with a bit of a beard. The man looked pretty sick to me. He was opening his mouth as if he was trying to shout.'

'So that's it,' breathed Biggles. 'Let's get out. He's watch-
ng us. We'll talk about this when we get outside. See me
rough.'

Biggles climbed into his seat.

Bertie walked on to the opening in the wall.

CHAPTER 12

AN UNEXPECTED HAZARD

USING hand signals, Bertie saw the *Merlin* through the gate way to the open ground outside, and having helped Biggle to line up in the direction of take-off to cover the same trac they had used when landing, climbed into his seat.

'What are you going to do?' he asked in a troubled voice

'I don't know,' answered Biggles slowly. 'It needs think ing about.'

'O'Connor must be holding someone prisoner.'

'Not necessarily, but he could be.'

'If he is, it could only be Browning.'

'It may be that Browning was injured in the crash an Connor is taking care of him.'

Bertie looked doubtful. 'You don't really believe that?'

'Frankly, no. If it was as simple as that there would hav been no need for Connor to lie – unless, of course, he' playing some dirty game of his own.'

'Why not have it out with Connor right here and now?'

'And start a rough house? That doesn't seem a ver bright idea to me. I know my limitations when it comes to punch-up. If that big tough went for us we should end up b needing hospital treatment. He'd only have to knock a hol in our machine to keep *us* here. Oh no. I'm not taking an chances on that.'

'We shan't know the truth unless we can get to this man i the fort.'

'I realize that. But the last way we'd be likely to succeed would be by going back in there and having a show-down with Connor. I'm not saying he's a villain. He might be. He might not. We don't know, although from what we've been told, his reputation in Windhoek isn't too good. From what I've seen myself, he isn't the sort of man I'd care to upset, particularly if he'd had a few drinks. In a scrap, with those big fists of his, he'd make mincemeat of us. Do *you* feel like taking him on?'

'No, thank you very much.' Bertie was emphatic. 'What shall we do, then?'

'When in doubt, do nothing in a hurry. I think our best plan would be to go somewhere nice and quiet and think about it. If possible find a place under cover from where we can see the fort and wait for Connor to go out in his jeep. If he'll go out, we can go in. For a start, the thing is to make him believe we've gone back to Windhoek. That should put his mind at rest if he has any reason to be afraid of the police uncovering something he'd rather they didn't see. I've no doubt he's still keeping an eye on us – probably wondering what we're sitting here nattering about.'

'Okay, old boy, let's do that,' agreed Bertie. 'How about going to roost for a little while on the far side of that big stretch of scrub and stuff? It isn't too close and it isn't too far away.'

'I was thinking the same thing.' Biggles paused. 'You know,' he went on reflectively, 'there's still something about this whole business that has got me foxed. These confounded rubies, which are really the kernel of the nut. Where are they? Has Browning still got them? Has Connor got them, or is he scheming to get them? Without them we've no case against either Browning or Connor, so if we tried any high-handed stuff we might find ourselves in the wrong. You know as well as I do that in cases of wrongful arrest, people always take sides against the police. But let's get away from here for a start.' Biggles' hand moved to the throttle.

The machine moved forward, slowly, then faster. The tail lifted, and in a minute the *Merlin* was kicking the hot atmosphere behind it in a steady climb.

'Connor is still in the yard. He's watching us go,' observed Bertie, glancing below and behind.

'Fine. I hope he's satisfied. I fancy he has more brawn than brains, or he wouldn't be so naïve as to suppose we'd believe his story that a plane could crash on his doorstep without him knowing anything about it. It'd smoke for days, and we know he must have been there, or the water put out for the leopard would have evaporated.'

Biggles held the plane on its course, still climbing slowly, until from some way behind the scrub he was satisfied he could no longer be seen from the fort. Then, after a slow turn, he cut the engines and glided back towards the broad belt of scrub and mixed dwarf timber. 'Let me know if you see anything likely to get in our way,' he said, as he himself surveyed the ground in front and below them.

'Looks all clear to me,' reported Bertie.

'And me. Let's try it.'

Presently the wheels were rumbling. The machine took rather a long run in the thin air to settle down, but finally it came to a standstill not far from the straggling fringe of the scrub. Biggles took it a little nearer and switched off. 'This should do us,' he said. 'I hope she won't take any harm standing in the sun.' There was no shade to speak of. He stood up to see if there was a gap under the trees wide enough to take the machine. There was not. 'We shall be able to get a clear view of the fort from the far end,' he went on. 'We shall have to walk it. I daren't take the machine any closer that way; as it is we shall have to take a chance on Connor coming in this direction. If he does we shall have to pretend we've had to make a forced landing.'

'There doesn't appear to be much in the way of game to bring him here.'

'Maybe not, but apparently Connor sometimes comes this way. I'm not forgetting that it must have been somewhere near here that he – I don't see how it could have been any-one else – took a shot at us. He brought a deer home with him this morning, so he's got some meat to go on with.'

Biggles got out and stamped on the ground. Satisfied that the surface was the same as it had been in the vicinity of the fort – hard-packed gravel – he lit a cigarette and walked on to the nearest tree, a mimosa with a flat top, to take advan-tage of what little shade it offered. Bertie joined him.

'We're in no great hurry,' Biggles said. 'We may have to wait some time for Connor to go off on another hunting trip, or whatever he's doing. Presently we'll move a bit nearer the fort and watch if the jeep goes out. I don't suppose Connor does much walking.' He sat down at the foot of the tree.

He did not remain seated for very long. A sudden crash in the dense undergrowth behind him brought him to his feet. 'What the devil was that?' he ejaculated.

'Sounded to me like an elephant blundering about,' Bertie said. 'Are there any elephants here?'

'I suppose there might be, but I wouldn't think so unless there's a water-hole somewhere in this rough stuff. This doesn't look like elephant country. They usually roam about in herds, anyway, although an old rogue might be on his own. I doubt if there's enough feed here for an elephant. With his bulk he has to eat eighteen hours a day to keep alive.'

'I can still hear it, whatever it is,' Bertie said, trying to see into the thicket. 'It seems to be coming this way, too,' he concluded anxiously.

'Not to worry,' returned Biggles casually. 'If by some chance there should be an elephant in the offing he's not likely to interfere with us. He'd be more likely to keep clear, particularly if Connor has been in the habit of shooting any-where near here.'

He was about to resume his seat when a crashing of twigs not far away caused him to change his mind.

'Oh my sainted aunt!' exclaimed Bertie, who was looking along the side of the jungle. 'Look what's here!'

Biggles turned his head to look. About fifty yards distant, standing on the border of the wood, staring out across the open ground in an aggressive attitude, was a rhinoceros, an old bull from the size of his horn. Three tick-birds pecked about on its back.

Bertie backed a pace nearer the only cover available.

'Keep still, you ass,' hissed Biggles. 'What do you think you're going to do with that?' he went on cuttingly, as Ber-tie took out his pistol. 'Put it away.'

It seems likely that the tick-birds heard this. Or they may have spotted the two men. At all events they took wing, uttering their warning cries. The rhinoceros got the message. He snorted. He advanced a pace, head up, staring at the desert. He looked left. He looked right. He twirled his little tail. His whole attitude indicated trouble if he could find it.

'Don't move,' breathed Biggles. 'He may not see us. Rhino's have poor vision. If he doesn't wind us he may move off.'

'If he decided to take it out of the machine we've had it, chum.'

'Still.'

The rhino trotted a few yards into the open, blowing froth. He blinked about like a short-sighted man trying to see where he is. He sniffed loudly, putting more faith in his sense of smell.

Biggles and Bertie might have been statues.

For a minute it looked as if all would be well. The tick-birds returned to the back of their host and resumed their quest for grubs. Then the most abominable luck took a hand. Bertie sneezed. He tried to hold it back, but all this did was produce a muffled explosion. That did it. The birds leapt into the air. The rhino jumped as if he had been stung.

'He's coming,' gasped Bertie.

'Get up a tree.'

The rhino, after running in circles, charged into the desert on a course that looked as if it would bring him into collision with the aircraft, which he may or may not have seen. By this time Bertie was shinning up the tree at a speed he could not have thought possible. Throwing a leg over the first branch, feeling reasonably safe, he looked to see what was happening. At the spectacle that met his eyes he nearly fell. The rhino was charging towards the plane and Biggles was running after it. With his eyes saucering he paused to watch this unbelievable performance.

The rhino, appearing not to know what it was doing, missed the tail of the plane by a yard and blundered on some little distance before it stopped, stamping its feet and dripping saliva as it glared around for whatever in its blind rage it had hoped to find and destroy. By this time Biggles had reached the machine. He jumped in, and without stopping to close the door dived into his seat. The starter whirred. The engines came to life with a roar and a spurt of blue smoke from the exhausts. The plane moved forward. The movement, of course, caught the rhino's eyes. That was all he needed. He charged flat out.

Bertie ceased to breathe, for it seemed that the beast must overtake the object of its fury, which of necessity could at first only move slowly. But it gathered speed every second, and the animal, not having the wit to make allowances for a moving target, thundered past the tail unit, missing the mark by a couple of yards. Bertie breathed again. The aircraft was now travelling tail up. It did not stop. The rhino did a circle apparently mystified by its disappearance. He caught the reek of its wake of exhaust gas, stopped and squealed. This seemed too much for the already bewildered animal. He set off at a gallop across the desert. This time he did not stop, but went on until he was a diminishing object in the distance.

Biggles, who had not left the ground, must have observed the rhino's departure, for he made a wide turn and taxied slowly back to the original position.

Bertie dropped from his tree. 'By gosh! old boy. You put the wind up me,' he declared earnestly.

'I put the wind up myself,' admitted Biggles. 'I'm out of practice for this sort of frolic. It's time we remembered where we are instead of behaving as if we were at an airport.'

'A bit unusual, wasn't it, for a rhino to behave like that without the slightest provocation?'

'Maybe he had a reason. Something must have upset him. The thought that we were going to lose the machine upset me, too. I could see only one hope of saving it.'

'I'm wondering what else there may be in this bally jungle.'

'So am I. Where did the rhino come out? There may be a track. Let's have a look.' Biggles walked along the edge of the scrub to the spot where the animal had emerged. He stopped, pointing at the ground. 'Ah! I thought that might be it. Can you see what I see?'

Bertie looked down. 'Blood.'

'That's the answer. It's not surprising the big brute was annoyed. It was wounded. Someone must have had a shot at it.'

'Connor.'

'I don't see how it could have been anyone else. He's a professional hunter. He was after the horn, no doubt. Rhino horn is nearly worth its weight in gold in China as a potent medicine, for which reason the rhino was well on its way to extinction before the poachers were stopped. Of course, the racket still goes on. Maybe that's why one came here looking for a hideout. I have an idea the rhinos are now on the protected list. If so, it looks as if Connor, apart from anything else he might be, makes a bit on the side by poaching. Let's go back to the plane. I need a drink after this.'

'And then what?' asked Bertie, looking apprehensively at the scrub as they made their way back to the aircraft.

'We'll stick to our original plan and stay here for a while. Why not? The only thing is, I'd feel happier if we had a weapon a bit heavier than an automatic pistol. That old rhino has given me a different idea about what we might encounter in this half-baked forest. It's the only piece of cover for miles. There might be anything in it; and as far as big game is concerned, a pistol is about as much use as a pea-shooter. We should have brought a rifle, but I wasn't thinking of anything like this. I wouldn't mind so much in the ordinary way. But if we're going to have wounded animals to contend with, it's a different matter altogether.'

They reached the plane and refreshed themselves with a cool drink of sparkling soda water, a few bottles of which had been put on board to prevent the risk of picking up a virus from surface water that in hot climates is so often polluted.

'Are you thinking of staying the night here?' questioned Bertie.

'I haven't yet made up my mind about that,' Biggles answered. 'There are arguments for and against. But as we're here we might as well hang on for a bit to see if anything happens at the fort.'

'I was thinking . . .'

'Thinking what?'

'If Connor is holding Browning a prisoner we'd better not wait too long before we do something about it. I mean to say, after what has happened today, if Connor gets the idea we're likely to stick around looking for Browning ... well, he might ...'

Biggles nodded. 'I see what you mean. I'm afraid that's a risk we shall have to take. We can't be certain that the man you saw *was* Browning. Even if he was, it doesn't mean he's a prisoner. He might be hiding up, for which he has a good reason. I'm still puzzled about that pile of stones. I would have sworn it was a grave, and I was fully prepared to find Browning in it. I could be wrong. It was a pity Connor came back just in time to prevent us from investigating. Meanwhile, now we've got our breath back, it would be a good moment to have a snack from the grub locker. Having done that, we'll move along and find a place from which we can watch the fort to see if Connor goes out.'

'That's not a bad idea. Something tells me a spot of tuck is indicated.'

Bertie was handing out a packet of biscuits and a tin of sardines when from a distance, in the direction of the fort, there came the crack of a rifle shot. He turned questioning eyes to Biggles' face. 'That was a shot.'

'I heard it. Good. It tells us Connor is still there.'

'I'm not so sure you're right when you call it good. That might have been Connor getting rid of Browning by putting a bullet through him.'

'I think it's more likely he's decided to waste no more time feeding his leopard, so he's done away with it. When we go back I fancy we shall find its collar empty.'

'Do you mean he'd shoot the poor beast on its chain?'

'What else could he do?'

'Let it go.'

'You might; but not Connor. If you ever see that skin again I'd wager someone else will be wearing it.'

'What a skunk the fellow must be,' growled Bertie.

'Never mind that. Hand out some grub,' requested Biggles impatiently. 'You're wasting time.'

CHAPTER 13

TENSE WORK BY MOONLIGHT

THE day wore on. Biggles and Bertie, having staved off hunger by drawing on their reserve store of iron rations, leaving the *Merlin* where it stood in the absence of anywhere better to put it, had made their way to the end of the area of scrub and there, just inside the sun-scorched fringe, had taken up positions from which the fort could be observed. They could not actually see the gateway entrance through the outer wall because that was on a side facing the wilderness, but they would be able to see if anyone left the place either on foot or in the jeep. It was some little distance away. Biggles would have preferred to be closer, but this would have meant crossing country where there was not a scrap of cover and so exposing themselves to anyone who happened to look in their direction.

The wall of the fort that faced them was blank except for three unglazed windows in the upper storey. Their original purpose may have been to serve as loopholes should the fort be attacked. Biggles hoped they would not find it necessary to walk to the fort. His intention was to wait for Connor to go out, when they would use the *Merlin* as a conveyance, taxiing across the open. This was the plan, although there was, of course, some doubt about Connor leaving the place.

The sun was now well past its zenith, and in the dry heat without a sign of life the waiting became tedious.

'If we're going home in daylight we shall soon have to be moving,' Bertie remarked.

'The trouble is, if we leave the place, that is, go now and come back in the morning, we shan't know if Connor is in or away. He might leave early, about dawn, before it gets too hot.'

'If you're going to look at it like that we might sit here until we have blisters on our bottoms.'

Biggles did not answer.

Time passed. The sun, a monstrous ball, was soon resting on the horizon. Through the thin air, from somewhere in the distance came a vibrant, deep-throated rumble.

'Did you hear that?' asked Bertie.

'Not being deaf, of course I heard it.'

'No need to get irritable, old boy. That was a lion.'

'So what? It sounded miles away. Anyhow, it wouldn't be likely to interfere with us except in the unlikely event of it being a man-eater.'

'All the same, I prefer my lions behind bars.'

'It may do us a bit of good.'

'How do you work that out?'

'Connor might go out to have a crack at it. He's a professional hunter. His business is to collect skins.'

'I wouldn't care to bet on that.'

'I wouldn't care to bet on anything here. Anything could happen.'

'A nice cheerful thought, I must say.'

Silence fell. The sun had not much longer to live, as Bertie pointed out.

'No matter. It won't be long before the moon comes up.'

'I've got an idea.'

'Tell me.'

'Let's do something.'

'Such as what?'

'Try a spot of scouting.'

'That sounds a bit vague.'

'I'm getting browned off with squatting here doing nothing.'

'So am I, but I can see nothing else to do.'

After staring at the fort for some time, Bertie went on, 'I've been thinking. I don't see why we shouldn't get into the fort without using the gateway. Notice how in places the sand has drifted half-way up the walls. If you stood on my shoulders you should just about be able to reach one of those windows facing us.'

'The windows might have bars. We can't see that from here.'

'Is there any reason why we shouldn't have a closer look. It would give us something to do.'

'Aren't you forgetting something?'

'What?'

'A man named Connor. He probably beds down for the night in the fort. He's got a rifle. Your scheme strikes me as a nice easy way to get ourselves shot.'

'He wouldn't dare.'

'If you believe that you're a pretty poor judge of character. He's playing a deep game. I'm sure he has something to hide, and knowing we're police, he'll do anything to prevent us from finding out what it is. Take it from me: if he was on the level, at a place like this he'd be delighted to meet a couple of white men to pass the time of day with. Any ordinary man would have invited us to have a drink. Did he? Not on your life. He hated the sight of us, and didn't mind us knowing it. I'm not going out of my way to look for trouble. It may come to that, but let's avoid it if we can.'

Another silence. A moon three-quarters full climbed into the sky to begin its eternal journey across the heavens. Again the lion, still a long way off, sent its voice across the lonely waste. The larger stars began to light their lamps.

Without the sun the temperature of the thin air began to drop sharply.

'I call this a dull game played slow,' grumbled Bertie. 'Connor won't be going out tonight, that's for sure.'

'You're probably right.'

'Then how about taking a walk to see if those windows are barred? It's getting chilly sitting here.'

'All right. If you're feeling all that energetic I suppose we might as well. Connor is unlikely to go out at this hour of night. We may have been stupid to wait; but while it was light there was just a possibility.' Biggles got up.

They started off across the plain, now as still and silent as a frozen sea, gleaming like old silver in a flood of moonlight. Unlike the great sand deserts farther north, there were no dunes to cast shadows. Only the black silhouette of the fort stood out clear and sharp. The silence was absolute; of an intensity no longer to be found in civilized parts of the world. It discouraged conversation. In such conditions any sound, however slight, would be magnified and heard at a distance.

They reached the fort, which here, as already stated, formed part of the outer wall. That is to say, they were confronted by the rear of the old barracks, whereas previously they had only seen the building from the front; from the courtyard or parade ground. Here, as Bertie observed, the windblown sand of years had piled up, in places half-way to the windows, the only means of gaining an entrance. The moonlight had not yet reached this side of the building, so even standing below the windows it was still not possible to see if they were barred. They appeared merely as square black holes.

Instinctively dropping his voice, Biggles said: 'If you'll give me a bunk up I'll see if it's possible to get in. You wait here.' As he made a final survey of the open ground behind them his fingers closed on Bertie's arm. 'Ssh,' he whispered.

Bertie looked quickly to see what it was that had engaged Biggles' attention. Across the moonlit desert, moving towards the fort from the forest was a small dark object. It appeared to bowl over the ground for a distance and then rise up to look around before continuing its progress.

'What the devil is it?' whispered Bertie.

'What do *you* make of it?'

'Is it a hyena?'

'I don't think so. I've never heard of hyenas standing on their hind legs, but I suppose they could if they had a reason.'

'Could it be some sort of ape? A gorilla or a chimpanzee.'

'I don't think they come as far south as this. They occur in real forest country and I certainly wouldn't expect to find any in the Kalahari. I can only think it must be a Bushman, although what he's doing I wouldn't have a clue. He seems to be scared of something.'

'Surely it's too small to be a human being?'

'Bushmen are undersized people, little more than pygmies.'

Together they watched the creature reach the fort, eventually to disappear from view as it passed beyond the end of the building against which they stood.

'It must have been a Bushman,' Biggles said. 'I don't see how it could have been anything else.'

'Where do you suppose he's gone?'

'How could I know? He was certainly making for the fort. Where else could he be going? Maybe he needed water and reckoned on finding some there. We know there must be water somewhere inside. I'm wondering why he came as he did, as if he was stalking something. Moreover, he was alone. According to my information, these people travel in tribes, or at least in family parties.'

'Perhaps he was scared of bumping into Connor. I seem

to remember Carter saying something about rumours that
he knocked them about; that sort of thing, if you see what I
mean. Is that why he carries a whip?'

Biggles brushed the problem aside with an impatient
shrug. 'What does it matter? The natives are no concern of
ours.'

'As long as they don't interfere with the plane.'

'I can't think of any reason why they should. They're
harmless, or so we've been told. We've done nothing to upset them, and should we meet any I shall take care not to.
But instead of standing here nattering, let's get on with what
we came to do. All I want to know is the name of the man
whose face you saw at the window. It may be Browning. If it
isn't we shall have to start looking somewhere else, although
between you and me I'm getting a bit cheesed off with this
whole business. Even if we find Browning, if he hasn't got
the rubies on him we shan't be able to prove anything. If he
has we can't arrest him here, so what's the point of it? I
knew when we started that the best we could hope for was
find out the truth about the rubies; but if Browning is dead,
or possibly being kept there against his will, it becomes a
different matter. Give me a lift up.' Biggles stood flat against
the wall, arms upraised, one leg out behind him.

Bertie took hold of the leg and hoisted. Biggles was just
able to reach the window. He pulled himself up and looked
down. 'It's barred,' he reported. 'Stand fast.'

Just above the window was one of the gaps in the cas-
tellated wall. Holding one of the window bars in his left
hand, he reached up with the other and got a grip on the
masonry. Raising the other hand, it was a fairly simple matter to pull himself up. A final heave and he was standing on
the flat roof. Seeing nothing of interest, he walked quietly
across to the far side. He was now overlooking the supposed
parade ground. There was no one in sight. Not a movement.
Not a sound. He saw the jeep. It had been parked in the

open gateway. What was the idea of that? Biggles wondered. Was it to make sure that the plane, or any other vehicle, could not get in? At any rate not without the jeep being moved, which would involve a certain amount of noise, which in the silence would not fail to be heard. Connor didn't intend to be taken by surprise. Was that the answer?

Biggles did not waste time in speculation. Where was Connor? That was the most important thing. As the jeep was there, it was reasonable to suppose he was not far away. But where? Without knowing where the man was, it looked as if nothing had been gained by the rooftop reconnaissance. Without that information, to look for the man whose face Bertie had seen at the window would be a hazardous enterprise, to say the least. If he encountered Connor what possible excuse could he give for snooping about in the fort?

Biggles considered the situation. It was a matter of common sense that if the crenellated wall had been built for defence, with the roof commanding an all-round view of the desert, there must obviously be a means of reaching it from the inside of the fort. Where was it? It would be a good thing to know, if not for the present then for some future occasion.

He began quietly to move along the roof, looking for an opening, a trap door or something of the sort. While doing this a movement in the courtyard below caught his eye. When he looked it had stopped, and he had to concentrate for some seconds before he caught sight of it again. Without a sound it was creeping along the opposite side of the courtyard. The far side from where he stood, not yet touched by direct moonlight. By its shape he recognized it for the creature that had come across from the wood. When it rose erect he saw his guess had been right. It was a small, almost miniature native. It could only be a Bushman. So he had come into the yard. For what purpose? Biggles did not

waste time trying to guess. He watched until the creature
had merged into the gloom at the far end of the yard, near
the crashed plane.

Dismissing the incident from his mind as having no importance, Biggles went on, looking for an entrance to the
interior of the fort which he felt sure must be there. If he
needed confirmation it came when he stepped on something
hard. He picked it up. It was a spent cartridge case. Brass.
Clearly, if a rifle had been fired from the roof someone had
been there, so there must be a way up.

He had to go to the extreme end of the building before he
found it. A hole. Just a hole in the roof. A hole about two
feet square. There was no trap door. If there had ever been
one it had gone; been removed or rotted away in the years
since the fort had been abandoned. A slant of moonlight
revealed a flight of steep, almost vertical, stairs leading
down. Even by flickering on his petrol lighter he couldn't
see the bottom, but it was reasonable to suppose they ended
in a room or corridor on the floor below.

Having found what he was looking for, he hesitated.
Should he go down or leave well alone? Without a torch to
see what he was doing, what could he do if he went down?
The risks were obvious. The last thing he wanted at this stage
was a collision with Connor, who could not be far away.
The purpose of his being there would be all too obvious, and
Connor could be expected to resent being spied on. Biggles
looked around. The place was as silent as a tomb. Common
sense counselled a return to Bertie forthwith; but to do that,
he reasoned, might mean losing an opportunity to make
contact with the unknown occupant. After reflection, he decided that having come so far he might as well take advan-
tage of his position and make an effort to see the business
through. It would have to be done some time, if not now. If
he retired he would have to return sooner or later. Anyway,
he resolved to go as far as the bottom of the stairs, if no

arther. His petrol lighter would give sufficient light to show
him anything there was to see.

Approaching the stairs with the caution the occasion demanded, lighter in hand, he started down. As his full weight
fell on them calamity struck in a manner he least expected.
The step on which he stood, rotted perhaps by long ex-
posure to the weather, collapsed. The next instant the entire
staircase crashed down with a noise sufficient – to use the
well-worn expression – to awaken the dead. Clutching for
support where there was none, he went down in the wreckage.

BERTIE TAKES A CHANCE

IT was fortunate for Biggles that he had not far to fall; a matter of no more than eight to ten feet; and while he was not seriously hurt, as he quickly ascertained, the breath was knocked out of him and he was badly shaken by shock, so sudden was the accident. He leaned against a wall, a stone wall by the feel of it, to recover.

As the echo of the noise subsided, the first thought that occurred to him was he had announced his presence in no uncertain manner. To hope that such a din had not been heard by anyone and everyone, both in and outside the building, would be optimism to the point of being ridiculous. The effect was a foregone conclusion. Through the hole above him faint moonlight showed he was in a passage. That was all. The light did not extend far enough to provide any further information, although a small patch of blue light some distance along showed the position of one of the windows, one that overlooked the courtyard. He listened. And with what anxiety he listened can be imagined.

He heard a sound, and it was one that did not surprise him. Footsteps. Approaching. Echoing along the stone passage. He looked up, and for the first time the full extent of the disaster dawned on him. There was no staircase. The whole thing lay at his feet in a heap of rotten and splintered woodwork. Above, a square of star-besprinkled sky looked down at him. It was well out of reach. Obviously there could be no

scape that way. To get out he would have to go down. Then
and the only exit. The main door. As he was on the upper
floor there must be a way down, he thought desperately, for
the footsteps were coming nearer. Where were the steps?
Still breathing heavily from his fall, on tiptoe he started
groping his way along the corridor, hoping to find a flight of
steps or stairs; he moved away, of course from the sound of
the approaching footsteps. He reached the window. It was
barred with iron rods. No getting out that way. Just beyond
it, on the opposite side, was an opening. It turned out to be a
small room. There was no door. Actually it was no more
than a cubicle. There was nothing in it except a narrow rusty
iron bedstead, pushed against the far wall, which suggested
that in the distant past it had been an officer's quarter.

The footsteps were now so loud, preceded by the light of a
torch, that he dare go no farther for fear of being seen. So he
backed into the room and kept still. He heard the footsteps
stop, and not daring to risk a peep, waited.

He judged when the footsteps stopped that the man
coming down the corridor had reached the collapsed staircase. With a little imagination Biggles could visualize him
surveying the wreckage and wondering what had caused it.
Would he guess the truth? He might. He might not. Rotten
wood can fall without human agency. It was an anxious
moment; a brief period, brittle with possibilities. Should the
man come on, having a torch, Biggles in his doorless little
cubicle would inevitably be discovered. That would mean a
show-down, if nothing more serious. He was not prepared
for that – not yet. He would have preferred his own time and
place when it came – if it had to come.

Then, as he stood there prepared for the worst, to his
great relief he heard the footsteps receding. Knowing the
man must now be facing the other way, he risked a quick
peep. What he saw was what he expected. It was Connor. He
got a glimpse of him as he passed a window. It seemed incon-

ceivable that there could be two men of such a build in the
fort. He had a jacket thrown over pyjamas and carried a
rifle.

Biggles breathed again. He waited for the footsteps to
fade to silence and then continued on his way along the
corridor, still looking for a way down. The passage ended in
a blank wall, apparently the extreme end of the building;
and there, in its most natural place, was a flight of stone
steps, descending. He groped his way down to discover that
the steps ended in another corridor, now obviously on the
ground floor. There was no outside door, and to make a
long story short he had to walk nearly the full length of the
building to reach the doorway which he knew was there,
having seen it from the courtyard on his first visit. However,
with windows at intervals in the outer wall, barred, of
course, he had no great difficulty in reaching his objective;
nerves at full stretch expecting any moment to be chal-
lenged.

He looked out, to left and right, at the moon-drenched
courtyard. All was quiet. Not a soul in sight. He went out,
and keeping tight against the wall hurried towards the main
exit from the fort.

As he did this there was a minor incident. He heard a faint
twang like a banjo string being stroked. This was followed
by another slight sound as if someone had thrown a pebble.
Seeing no one, he paid little attention to it at the time (although he was to remember it later) but hurried on, only too
glad to see a way out of his predicament. Not until he had
passed the jeep parked in the gap in the wall did he glance
back. The only thing to catch his eye was a feeble yellow
light in one of the upstairs windows. Feeling he had done
enough exploring for one night, he went quickly on his way
to the rear of the fort where he had left Bertie. He was still
there, still in the same place, gazing up at the roof.

When Biggles came up silently and spoke, he started as if

had been stung. 'Oh here, I say, don't give me shocks like at,' he protested. 'Where the devil have you just sprung om?'

'Sprung is the word.'

'You've been a heck of a long time.'

'I've been busy.'

'I expected you back the way you went.'

'So did I, but it didn't work out like that. Don't rush me, et me get my breath.'

'Have you seen Browning?'

'No. Hold hard while I light a cigarette. I need one to eady –' Biggles, who was feeling in a pocket, broke off bruptly.

'What's wrong?' asked Bertie, sensing something was miss.

'Drat it,' muttered Biggles. 'I've made a really bright oob.'

'What have you done?'

'Left my lighter in the fort. I had a fall. I was in the dark. I emember now the lighter was in my hand. I must have ropped it, and in the shock forgot all about it. I might not ave been able to find it anyway; but if in daylight Connor ots it, he'll realize someone has been inside. He must now I had a lighter because I lit a cigarette with it while we ere talking in the yard. Pity about that, but there it is. I'll ll you all about it presently. Have you got a match on ou?'

Bertie produced a box.

Biggles lit a cigarette. 'Thanks. Has anything happened ere?'

'Not a bally thing; but there's one thing I must tell you, hat confounded rhino has come back.'

'Come back where?'

'To the wood – I think.'

Biggles frowned. 'Are you sure about this?'

'No doubt about it. I watched it saunter back across th
desert.'

'Then it couldn't have been as badly wounded as we su
posed. Maybe it wasn't the same beast.'

'If it wasn't it was his twin brother. Of course I wouldn
swear it was the same brute. To me one rhino is like anothe
I suppose they can recognize each other, but to me they'
all alike. But tell me, what have you been doing?'

'Let's take the weight off our feet,' Biggles said, sitting c
the sand. 'With nothing urgent on hand we might as well re
here until it starts to get light. It'd be safer than ris
bumping into that damned rhino in the dark. By the wa
have you heard any more of that lion?'

'Not a squeak.'

'Good. Then let's hope he hasn't come this way to con
plicate things. Now I'll tell you about the daft game I'v
been playing.'

Having plenty of time, Biggles was able to tell in detail th
story of his nocturnal adventure.

'So where does that leave us, if you see what I mean?' sai
Bertie when he had finished.

'I wish I could tell you. The answer is, I suppose, it's
case of as we were. The only useful piece of information I'v
gathered is we can get into the fort without going throug
the gateway. But I don't think it would be advisable to d
that while Connor is around. We'd better stick to our orig
inal plan and wait for him to go out.'

'That may mean waiting here for some time.'

'Can you make any better suggestion?'

'Frankly, no, although I must say it's going to be a bit of
bind.'

'For the moment we could take it in turns to snatch a sp
of shut-eye. We shall need to sleep some time.'

'Do you mean here?'

'Not necessarily. We could rest in the machine. Tha

hould be more comfortable for more reasons than one.
Ve'd also have the advantage of having some grub handy.
'm no use in the morning till I've had my cuppa. Let's walk
cross, rhino or no rhino. We can't have our actions dictated
y the local zoo specimens.'

'Never mind the zoo. What about Connor? If he happens
o look out he'll see us in the moonlight crossing the
pen.'

'We'll take a chance on that,' decided Biggles. 'When I
aw him he was in pyjamas. He must have to sleep once in a
vhile. If Connor comes after us it'll be in the jeep, and we
hall hear it. Let's go.'

They got up, and after a look round for possible danger,
et off across the wilderness towards the scrub behind which
hey had left the plane. They started at a fast pace, but when
requent glances behind showed they were not being pur-
ued, they slowed to a steadier walk. It took the best part of
a quarter of an hour to reach the nearest point of the sun-
parched forest. Here they paused to listen. They could not
yet see the aircraft as it was parked along the side, so they
urned left and continued on their way to the corner to get
round to it. There was no question of pushing a way through
the shrubs, many of which bristled with ferocious thorns.

Biggles was the first to reach the corner. He looked round
it before going on. He stopped dead. Throwing out a re-
straining hand, he took a quick pace back.

'What is it?' asked Bertie, more as a matter of interest
than with alarm.

'Look for yourself.'

'Nothing wrong, I hope.'

'Not yet,' returned Biggles grimly.

Bertie advanced and looked.

In the fading light of the now waning moon he saw the
plane, apparently as they had left it. But that was not all.
Standing quietly on the far side of the tail unit, head out

sniffing at it, was the great black bulk of an animal. Un
mistakably it was the rhinoceros. Or at any rate *a* rhi
noceros.

Bertie stepped back. 'Oh no,' he groaned in a voice of
suppressed anguish. 'A thousand times no. Not *that* again
It isn't true.'

In spite of himself Biggles had to smile; but it was a bleak
effort. 'Nothing was ever truer,' he murmured sadly.

'What are we going to do about it?'

'You tell me,' invited Biggles. 'Do you feel like driving it
away?'

'No. Not me. Definitely,' declared Bertie emphatically
'I've driven a lot of things in my time, but I draw the line at
rhinoceroses.'

'That's what I thought.'

'If he decides he doesn't like the smell of it he may wan-
der off.'

'On the other hand he may decide to taste it. He may even
decide to have a look inside the cockpit.'

'If the ugly brute tries anything like that we're up the
creek without a paddle. What are you going to do?'

'Me? I'm going to find a nice easy tree to climb in case he
comes this way.'

'But look here, I say, we shall have to do something.'

'If you imagine I'm going to tackle a ton of armour-
plated rhino meat with a pocket pistol it's time you had your
head examined,' stated Biggles coldly, again looking round
the corner. 'Hold hard,' he went on. 'What's he doing? He
seems to have fallen in love with an aeroplane.'

'What are you talking about?'

'He's lying down beside it.'

'Charming,' sneered Bertie.

'Well, at least that's better than sticking his horn into her.'

'I'll tell you what,' Bertie said. 'If someone started the
engines –'

'Who's going to start them?'

'I don't mind having a shot at it. If he's having a snooze it might be possible to . . . you get up a tree and watch. If you see me coming back in a hurry make room for me.'

'You're out of your mind.'

'Okay, so I'm out of my mind; but I'm not losing any more of my beauty sleep, and I'm certainly not going to doss down on ground that's crawling with all the bugs in creation.'

'He'll wind you before you get half-way.'

'As there's no wind he'll be clever to do that,' argued Bertie. 'I reckon if he spots me he'll bolt.'

'I wouldn't care to bet on that.'

'We'll see.' So saying, Bertie walked slowly round the corner, which brought him in view of the apparently sleeping animal. It did not move. He continued to advance, keeping close to the edge of the wood; and so he went on until he was directly opposite the plane and not more than twenty yards from it. Still the animal had not moved. It appeared to be sound asleep.

Never taking his eyes from it, step by step, ready to run for his life, Bertie began to cross the intervening gap, as far as possible keeping the machine between himself and the recumbent beast. In this way he reached the cabin door. Very quietly he opened it. Before getting in he stooped for a last look under the fuselage at the animal. It was still lying on its side. Suddenly it struck him that it was keeping unnaturally motionless. If it was breathing he thought he should at least see its flank moving. There was no such movement. No sound. Not the slightest. Then for the first time it slowly dawned on him that the monster might be dead. It was known to have been wounded. He hesitated, looking hard, listening intently.

Braced ready to spring into the aircraft at the first sign of life, he coughed gently. Coughed again, a little louder. This brought no response. He thought quickly. It seemed a pity to start the engines if there was no need. The sound would be heard by Connor and tell him they were there. He picked up a pebble. Tossed it. It fell on the animal. It did not move. He threw a larger stone. Nothing happened. Gaining confidence, but aware he was taking a risk, although a justifiable one, he moved to a position from which he had a clear view of the entire animal. Under its head a black stain was spreading over the dry earth. Blood. So that was it. The rhino *was* dead. It had come back to its homeground and there lain down to die.

Bertie drew a deep breath of relief. For the last several minutes he had been under considerable strain. Now, relaxed, he moved into the open and looked across to where he knew Biggles to be. He waved. 'He's dead,' he called.

Biggles came running. From a short distance he slowed down to regard the ponderous beast suspiciously. Seeing the blood, he came on. 'Jolly good show,' he congratulated. 'Full marks.'

'Thanks,' acknowledged Bertie. 'Never so scared in my life, but now perhaps we can snatch forty winks in peace.'

'Right. You get on with it,' Biggles said. 'You can have a couple of hours. I'll keep first watch – just in case.'

CHAPTER 15

BROWNING TELLS HIS TALE

BERTIE was awakened by Biggles shaking him gently by the shoulder. He got up quickly to see a new-born sun flooding the desert with streams of pink and gold. The rhino still lay where it had died.

'Listen,' Biggles said succinctly.

From the direction of the fort came the unmistakable sound of a motor vehicle. 'The jeep,' said Bertie.

'Yes. It has just been started. Connor must be going out. I thought I'd better wake you, to be ready in case he comes this way. Ah! there he goes. Thank goodness he's going in the opposite direction.' Biggles picked up the binoculars that lay handy.

The jeep had emerged from the fortress through the gap in the wall and without stopping carried on across the desert at an angle, apparently running along the shallow bed of what must have been a dried-up water course. It finally disappeared from sight, leaving a settling trail of dust to mark its passage.

'That's fine!' exclaimed Biggles. 'I can't see anyone with him. At the rate he's going, I think he must be going a fair distance. This is what we've been waiting for. Let's get cracking while the going's good.'

'Aren't we stopping for a cup of tea?'

'There's no time for that. It'll have to wait.'

'What if he comes back?'

'That's a chance we shall have to take. The fact that he's made such an early start suggests he's likely to be away for some time. Now we'll find out who else is in that barracks.'

'Are you going to walk over?'

'Not on your life. It'll be quicker to taxi across.' Biggles settled in his seat, started the engines, made a wide turn to clear the dead rhino and headed at a safe speed for the objective. 'Keep an eye on where Connor disappeared and let me know if you see him coming back,' he ordered.

'I'll watch it.'

A run of a few minutes across the open ground took them to the fort.

'Are you going to take her inside?' questioned Bertie.

'Not this time. We may want to leave in a hurry. It shouldn't take long to find out what we want to know.' Biggles switched off. Leaving the plane as it stood, just outside the entrance gateway, they walked through and were making for the open door of the fort itself when Biggles touched Bertie on the arm. No words were necessary. The chain that had secured the leopard cub was still there; but the animal was not.

'Never mind that,' Biggles said. 'At which window did you see the face?'

'The one at the end, top floor.'

They went on to the doorway. Bertie stooped and from the bottom of the wall picked up what was obviously a small arrow. 'I wonder how that got here?'

Biggles' eyes opened as he remembered the sounds he had heard overnight as he had left the building and now realized what had made them. 'Put it down,' he snapped. 'Scratch yourself with that and you'll have no further interest in Browning, or anyone else. Look at that muck on the point. I'd say that's poison.'

Bertie threw the arrow on the ground with an exclamation of disgust. 'What's it doing here?'

'Somebody took a shot at me last night.'

'Why you?'

'Maybe a Bushman thought I was Connor. Never mind that now. Let's get on.'

They went through the only entrance into the fort. Now, in daylight, Biggles could see that a passage ran both ways. 'I came down some steps at the far end,' he said. 'There should be some at this end.' He turned left along the corridor.

They hadn't far to go. They passed two large rooms which in the days when the fort was occupied by troops may have been dining or assembly halls, then came to a small one. Laid out on the floor to dry, still wet and bloody, was a leopard skin. 'There's your leopard,' Biggles said without stopping. A little farther on a flight of stone steps, matching those at the other end, mounted to the upper floor. At the top they found themselves in another corridor. Here were more cubicles, one, from some blankets and empty whisky bottles on the floor, looking as if it had recently been occupied. The corridor ended at a massive wooden door with an old-fashioned latch. It was shut.

Biggles banged on it with his fist. 'Anyone there?' he called.

A voice answered: 'Who is it?'

Biggles raised the latch, pushed the door open and walked in.

Sitting on an ancient iron bed on which lay some brown ex-army blankets, with a leg stuck out stiffly in front on him, was a man. He looked as if he had been ill. His face was pale and thin. His hair was long and unkempt and there was a stubble of beard on his chin. Nevertheless, Biggles recognized him at once from the photograph.

'You're Richard Browning,' he stated, rather than questioned.

'Quite right. Who are you?'

'We're police officers from London.'

A ghost of a smile flitted across Browning's face. 'So you managed to find me. What do you want?'

'We want the jewels belonging to Lord Langdon which you stole from his safe when you were employed by him.'

Browning shook his head. 'You're wrong on two counts. If you're talking of a certain collection of rubies they did not belong to Lord Langdon and I did not steal them. Do you happen to have a cigarette on you? I've run out.'

Biggles obliged. Bertie struck a match.

'Thanks,' said Browning. 'That's better. Sorry I can't ask you to sit down, but as you may have noticed we're a bit short of chairs.'

'We don't mind standing,' rejoined Biggles curtly. 'Look, Browning, you can't get away with this. You sold one of the rings to a jeweller in Bond Street.'

'I sold it at the request of the person who really owned it. What was wrong with that?'

'And you handed over the money, I suppose,' retorted Biggles cynically.

'I did.'

'Where did you get the money to buy a plane?'

'She put up the money for that.'

'She? Who are you talking about?'

'My sister. Or to be more correct, my half-sister. But of course you wouldn't know about that.'

'Suppose we stop beating about the bush,' requested Biggles. 'Who is this mysterious sister?'

'Lady Caroline Langdon.'

Biggles stared. 'Are you saying Lady Caroline is your *sister*?' he asked incredulously.

'Well, we both had the same father.'

'You mean – Lord Langdon?' Biggles seemed to have difficulty in getting the words out. Never had Bertie seen him so completely taken aback.

'That's what I said,' answered Browning calmly. 'Actually, if you want to get your facts right, I'd better tell you that my name is Langdon; the Honourable Richard Langdon, although I've never used the title.'

'Just a moment while I digest this,' Biggles said. He looked at Bertie. 'I told you there was a piece missing from the jigsaw. This is it.' Then, to Browning, 'But I understand you were employed at Ferndale Manor as a footman!'

'So I was.'

'How did that come about?'

'My father, not having seen me since I was a baby, had no idea who I was. It suited me not to tell him. It's a long story.'

'I'd like to hear it,' Biggles said. 'But what about Connor? Is he likely to come back?'

'I wouldn't think so. I imagine he's gone digging for diamonds. He went in the jeep. We shall hear it if it comes back.'

'What's your position here? Is he keeping you prisoner?'

'He has no need to keep me. He knows I can't get away. I had an accident and broke a leg. It's mending, but I couldn't walk a hundred yards without crutches. Connor knows that. He knows I depend on him for food and water.'

'You broke a leg when you crashed?'

'Yes. We had a row. We're still hardly on speaking terms.'

'How did this happen?'

'I'd better start at the beginning. I've nothing to hide, and as I see it I've done nothing to be ashamed of. When Lord Langdon was a young man – I'm talking about more than thirty years ago – he married my mother. He met her in South Africa while on a hunting trip. She was the only daughter of a South African mining magnate. I'm pretty sure he married her for money. He never had any to speak of. They went to his place in England, where I was born. He turned out to be a rotter, a brute and a spendthrift. He made my mother's life a hell. She stuck it for two or three years; then she left him and went back to South Africa, taking me with her. That's where I was brought up. They never saw each other again. He didn't care. He did nothing – he didn't even make her an allowance – until he wanted to marry again and through his lawyers wrote asking for a divorce, which my mother was only too glad to give him. By this time I was old enough to understand these things.'

'So Lord Langdon married again.'

'Yes. Another woman with money, of course. This time he had a daughter, Caroline. I gather he treated his new wife as he had treated my mother. She didn't live long. She died of a broken heart, so Caroline told me. Well, my mother died. She left me what money she had. Not knowing what to do with myself I decided to go on *safari,* hunting and exploring, and eventually found myself in the Kalahari where I'd heard rumours of a lost city.'

'And that's how you met Connor?'

'Yes. At first we got on fine. I must say that as a big game hunter he knew his job, although his real business was prospecting for diamonds. He was convinced that somewhere in the Kalahari there must be diamondiferous gravel, or how did the Bushmen find them? Anyhow, I stayed with him. After a time things began to go wrong. He drank a lot, and when he'd had too much he became unbearable. He treated the Bushmen like animals; knocked them about, swearing they knew where to find diamonds. I got fed up with this and decided to leave him.'

'Did he find any diamonds?'

'Not at this time. We had a gentleman's agreement that if we struck diamonds we'd go fifty-fifty. After all, the skin hunting business didn't pay off too well and I was grub-staking him. Maybe that's why he played hell when I told him I was packing up. What decided me to go to England I really don't know. I suppose it was in my blood to want to see the old country. Then a curious thing happened. Life can play strange tricks. When I was in London, looking through a newspaper I saw a notice, put in by Lord Langdon, advertising for a footman. On the spur of the moment, thinking it would be interesting to see my father and the ancestral home, I went down and applied for the job under the name of Browning; and to my surprise I got it.'

'You didn't let your father know who you really were?'

'Of course not. He still doesn't know. I wanted to see just what sort of a man he was. That didn't take me long. He's a bully. The sort of man who enjoys hurting people. I suppose that's why he enjoys killing animals. I was already thinking of leaving when complications arose. Not so much with him as with Caroline. What happened may have been my fault. She was always under his thumb and led a pretty miserable life. Blood being thicker than water, I was sorry for her and we spent too much time together. When she seemed to be getting too fond of me I decided it had to stop. Not knowing the truth, she suggested we ran away together and got married. I had to tell her that was impossible, and why.'

'You told her who you were?'

'Exactly. In a way that defeated its object because it only brought us closer together, although on a different footing. When I saw that Lord Langdon was getting suspicious of our relationship, I decided to get out. But there was one thing that worried me. My father was fast getting through what money he had. He had sold the farms, cut the timber, and the place was mortgaged to the hilt. Not only that, he was beginning to sell the jewels he kept in the safe. They weren't his. The rubies were Caroline's. They were left to her by her mother. Caroline told me about this. She knew where the key was kept and from time to time when her father was out she looked in the safe. It was obviously only a

question of time before all the rubies had gone the way of
the rest, in which case she was likely to be left penniless.'

'So you decided to take a hand?'

'Yes. What would you have done? Left your sister to the
mercy of a callous brute? Always having had a hankering to
be a pilot, I'd been taking flying lessons at a nearby club,
and this gave me the idea for a scheme to save Caroline's
rubies. You know what I did.'

'You said you didn't steal the rubies.'

'I merely took them out of the safe. That's a very different
matter.'

'Did Caroline know what you intended to do?'

'No, but she may have suspected. I told her I'd write to
her after I'd gone. So I moved the rubies and bolted, making
it look as if they'd been stolen and I was the thief. I didn't
think my father would call in the police.'

'He was a bit chary about it,' admitted Biggles.

'I wrote to Caroline as I promised. She knows where the
rubies are. I don't suppose she'll touch them. She has no use
for them at the moment, but this will prevent Lord Langdon
from getting his hands on them. I suppose you want me to
tell you where they are?'

Biggles thought for a moment. 'No, I think, for the time
being at any rate, I'd rather not know.'

'Why not?'

'Because if I know where they are I shall have to return
them to your father pending inquiries. Caroline is not yet of
age. Now I understand why she told me there was no question of you ever being married. The picture becomes clearer
every moment. What made you come back here?'

'To tell the truth I don't know,' answered Browning
frankly. 'I suppose it was because I didn't know where else
to make for; I wanted a place where I thought I could disappear for a time.'

'So you rejoined Connor?'

'Yes. That was a mistake. He could be a likeable fellow when he was sober, cheerful but unreliable. I thought perhaps after my absence he'd be tolerable. But he was worse. Seemed to have some sort of resentment against me for having left him. He was drinking more than ever. He greeted me by boasting that while I'd been away he'd struck a rich pan of diamonds, but he'd see me to hell before he'd share his find with me. While we were arguing, if you can call it an argument, because it's futile to argue with a man who's had too much to drink, a Bushman came in to ask if he could have some water. Connor cursed him, and when the wretched little man ran away he shot him as if he'd been a thieving jackal.'

Biggles frowned. '*Killed* him?'

'Stone dead. Then he dug a hole in the top end of the yard and threw the body in.'

'I saw the grave,' Biggles said. 'I thought you might be in it.'

'I could have been. I told Connor what I thought of him. When I piled some stones on the grave to beat the hyenas, he threatened to shoot me too. I decided I'd had enough. I'd put my plane in the yard facing the top end. When Connor saw I meant what I said, he stood in the gateway with his rifle and swore he'd shoot me if I tried to get through. I decided to get off without using the gate. I thought I just had enough room to clear the wall at the far end, and I think I would have done it had not Connor, realizing what I was doing, opened fire on me. By bad luck one of his bullets splintered one of the airscrews. I couldn't stop and crashed into the wall. I was knocked out. I can only think the shock must have sobered Connor because when I came round I was here, with a broken leg done up in home-made splints. He told me my plane had gone up in flames. I have a suspicion he set fire to it, knowing that without it I hadn't a hope of getting away.'

'But why was he so anxious to keep you here?'

'I fancy he had two reasons. First, I might report him for shooting the Bushman. Second, I might squeal about the diamonds. He's not likely to declare them to the police, as he should. It's my guess that when he's ready he'll push off and sell them to illicit buyers in the black market. When he goes, heaven knows what will happen to me. At all events, for the time being he's providing me with food and water.'

'Do you want to stay here?'

'Of course not, but there's nothing I can do about it.'

'We could take you to Windhoek, or even to England if you'd prefer it, although I should warn you that if you come home with us you might have to stand trial for taking the rubies.'

'I only moved them to a safe place. They belong to Caroline. She wouldn't prosecute me. She knows where they are. I wrote and told her.'

'You wrote care of someone in the village. I think I saw Caroline collect the letter.'

'If necessary she could produce the rubies to prove my innocence; that I only acted in good faith.'

'Lord Langdon might take you to court.'

'And rake up all his murky past? I don't think so.'

'Well, it's up to you. I haven't quite decided what my own position is in this queer set-up, but we'll get you to Windhoek for a start. You may have to spend some time there in hospital, to get your leg right, before talking of going anywhere else. If you're ready let's get out of this. We'll give you a hand. The sooner we're away the better. Connor may come back.'

'We shall hear the jeep,' said Browning, getting up and standing on one leg.

With his hands on their shoulders for support, Biggles and Bertie, not without some difficulty, got the injured man to the ground floor. After a short rest they moved on to the gateway.

As they approached, Connor, who must have been waiting outside the wall, stepped out, a sardonic smile on his face. A rifle lay across his arms, a finger through the trigger guard. 'And just where do you think you're going?' he inquired in a tone of voice that was both a jibe and a threat.

CHAPTER 16

CURTAINS FOR CONNOR

ON Connor's sudden and unexpected appearance, Biggles and his companions had naturally pulled up short, no doubt all equally astonished. Biggles looked for the jeep, but couldn't see it.

'It isn't here,' said Connor, apparently reading his thoughts. 'I walked back. That was my little trap. I guessed you'd be along. I knew you were here last night. You left something behind. I think this is yours. Catch.' Connor took a small object from his pocket and tossed it over.

Biggles caught it. It was his petrol lighter. 'Thanks,' he said evenly. 'I knew I'd dropped it.' He went on. 'We're taking Browning into Windhoek. He can't stay here in this state. He must have his leg properly set.'

'That's what *you* think,' sneered Connor. 'I've got other ideas.'

What these were was never disclosed, for at this juncture something occurred to put a very different aspect on the situation. It happened in a matter of seconds. It started with a faint *twang*. Connor started violently. Simultaneously, a small brown figure, bent double, dashed out of what had been the leopard den and raced twisting and turning for the exit. Connor moved nearly as fast. His rifle cracked, but a spurt of dust behind the Bushman showed the shot had missed. Before another shot could be fired the native was through the gateway and out of sight. Connor dashed after him. From outside came two reports. Then after a brief delay Connor reappeared. He seemed a little unsteady on his legs. 'Missed the little devil,' he growled. 'He got away down the *donga*.' (Dry river bed.) He stopped and felt at his neck from which projected several inches of what was obviously the shaft of an arrow. When his fingers closed over it his face turned white to the lips. 'Mother of God,' he breathed. With a curious air of resignation he threw his rifle on the ground. 'I shan't want that again,' he said.

'I'll take you into Windhoek,' Biggles said, realizing what had happened. 'There's plenty of room in my plane.'

'No use,' said Connor.

'The doctors should be able to do something.'

'Neither they nor anyone else can do anything about this,' stated Connor in a voice which in the circumstances seemed astonishingly calm. Never so quickly was a man the worse for drink struck sober.

'I wouldn't say that,' went on Biggles.

'Don't say anything.'

'But that's ridiculous. I can get you into Windhoek inside an hour.'

'Forget it. It's no use, I tell you. I know what I'm talking about. I can feel the poison in my blood already. Once that happens it's all over. I hope it won't take long. If the poison's stale it can take up to three days; but the end is always the same. Ah well! I suppose I asked for it,' concluded Connor with a quiet finality that few men faced with certain death could have muttered. 'It must have been a pal of that little rat I shot. They don't forgive or forget.'

'But let me –'

Connor broke in with, 'Don't waste your breath. I'll have a last drink, anyhow.' From his hip pocket he took a whisky flask, drank the contents and threw the flask on the ground.

'At least let me try to get the arrow out,' insisted Biggles.

'Why waste your time? I've known this stuff kill an eleph-

ant. I'm not worrying. I've had a fair run.' Connor looked at
Browning. 'Sorry if I was a bit rough with you, but I'm like
that. Here, take these. They won't be any use to me where
I'm going.' From his pocket he took a small leopard skin
bag about the size of a tobacco pouch and threw it over. As
Browning caught it the contents rattled. At the same time
Connor staggered and nearly fell. He walked slowly to the
wall and sat with his back against it. 'You'll find – the jeep –
up the *donga*,' he murmured in a voice that was becoming
blurred. 'Keep it. If you bury – me – here – remember – the
hyenas. It's getting – dark – early.'

'But look here, old boy, we can't just stand here and
watch him die,' burst out Bertie, looking at Biggles. 'I mean
to say . . .'

'I'm not going to,' declared Biggles. 'Whether he likes it
or not, I'm taking him to Windhoek. We'll get Browning in
first. Give a hand.'

Browning was helped into the aircraft. He was still holding the leopard skin bag.

'Do you want that?' asked Biggles. 'What's in it?'

'Diamonds.'

'I hope they bring you better luck than they've brought
Connor,' returned Biggles grimly.

On the way back to fetch Connor, Bertie said: 'Do you
believe Browning's story?'

'Every word of it,' answered Biggles. 'If I know anything
about men he couldn't have dreamed up a yarn like that. It
fits in with all we know.'

They returned to Connor to find him unconscious. With
considerable difficulty, for Connor was a heavy man, they
managed to get the limp body to the aircraft. It was even
more difficult to get him on the floor of the cabin.

'Is there absolutely nothing we can do?' said Bertie, in a
voice desperate with sympathy.

'Not a thing. He knew.'

In a matter of minutes the machine was on its way. But it turned out to be a wasted effort. By the time it reached the airport Connor was dead.

'Well, he got his last wish. He wanted the end to be quick,' remarked Biggles philosophically. 'I'll stay here with him. Go and phone the police and tell them to bring an ambulance for two. Then you'd better send a signal home to say we shall soon be on our way.'

'Okay.' Bertie hurried off.

Biggles kept vigil beside the dead man in the cabin. Browning sat with him. He was visibly upset. 'We spent a lot of time together,' he explained. 'If only he could have kept off the booze. When he was sober there was much about him to like. He never spoke about his past, but I sometimes had a feeling there was something he wanted to forget.'

'There are more sensible ways for a man to do that than try to drown it in whisky,' retorted Biggles. 'But who am I to talk? I tried it once, when I was young, and got shot down. Never again.'

Bertie returned, and a minute later a police ambulance roared up. It brought Carter, a sergeant and a medical orderly. 'What's all this?' demanded the sergeant, crisply.

'If you'll deal with these casualties we'll come along to the police station and tell you all about it,' Biggles said.

The sergeant took one look at Connor, the arrow still in his neck. All he said was: 'Ah! So he's got it at last. He's been asking for this for years.'

It turned out that Biggles had been over-optimistic in saying they would soon be on their way home. It was, in fact, three days before the police inquiry, which they had to attend, had finished its task and they were given permission to leave the country. Nothing was said about the rubies, the police only being interested in what had happened in their own territory; the deaths of Connor and the Bushman he had murdered; and, of course, the question of the diamonds Connor had found, which Browning had to hand over pending their valuation and ultimate disposal. Connor had no known relatives. As for Browning, having had his leg reset, he was still in hospital when the *Merlin* took off for home.

Even then, although Biggles had had ample time to think, and had succeeded in his purpose of finding Browning, he was still far from happy about the outcome of the affair, his sympathies being with Caroline and her brother whom they still called Browning. Nor was he sure what he was going to do when he reached home. On their last visit to Browning, in hospital, before leaving, he had asked him if he had any objection to Lord Langdon being told who he really was. To which Browning had replied he could tell him anything he liked. He couldn't care less. He was unlikely ever to see him again and had no wish to do so. 'You'll find me here if ever you want me.'

'That's how you feel now,' was Biggles' last word. 'You may feel differently should your father die and you decide to claim your inheritance.'

'I've still got my birth certificate,' Browning said.

Yet, as Biggles said to Bertie on the way home, it was all very difficult. 'I think the best thing is to tell the Air Commodore the entire story and leave the rest to him,' he concluded. 'We've done what he asked us to do.'

Bertie agreed.

CHAPTER 17

A FAMILY HATCHET IS BURIED

ON arrival at Scotland Yard, Biggles did what he had re-solved to do. He went to his chief, told him all that had happened and what he had learned.

'A strange story; but then, there's a lot in the old saying that truth is stranger than fiction,' commented the Air Commodore, tritely. 'How right you were when you said that neither Lord Langdon nor his daughter were giving us all the facts. You're satisfied that Browning was telling the truth?'

'I have no doubt about it. What had he to gain by fabri-cating such a fantastic story, knowing it could soon be proved or disproved?'

'True. We can soon settle that. Obviously there's only one thing to do now and that's tell Lord Langdon what you've learned and see how he feels about it. If it's the truth he's not likely to deny it. What action he decides to take, if any, will be up to him. I can't see him bringing a charge against his own children and so washing his dirty linen in public. He told us he was all against publicity and now we can see why. I fancy he'd prefer to see the whole business hushed up.'

Biggles nodded. 'So you'll go down and tell him?'

'I think it would be better for you to go. You've seen Browning and have the details at your finger-tips. He might ask some questions about his long-lost son, which I wouldn't be able to answer.'

151

'What if he demands the return of the rubies? I don't
know where they are. I told Browning I'd rather not know
where they were, or I might have tell his father. I saw no
reason why I should lie about it.'

'In my opinion this is now a family affair that will have to
be settled between Lord Langdon and his daughter. If she
can prove the jewels are her property Lord Langdon will
hardly dare to take them from her by force.'

'I'll put that to them,' Biggles said. 'You might ring up his
lordship and make an appointment for me for tomorrow
morning; say, about eleven. Tell him I have news for him.'

'News that should stop him worrying me on the telephone,' averred the Air Commodore. 'He seems to think we
have nothing to do except run around looking for his confounded rubies.'

'What I have to say should quieten him down,' Biggles
said, with a meaning smile.

The following morning at a little before eleven he presented himself at Ferndale Manor to keep an appointment
with Lord Langdon. He would have preferred to see Caroline, but there were obvious difficulties about this. He was
taken to the library where he found his lordship waiting
with an expression that was anything but inviting.

'It's about time you brought me some news,' he said
sourly.

'What I've brought may not be altogether welcome, my
lord,' returned Biggles coolly.

'What do you mean by that?'

'Had you been a little more frank the first time I came
here, it would have saved everyone time, and me, a lot of
trouble.'

'Indeed? What did I fail to tell you?'

'Several things. For instance, that you had previously
been married and that you had a son living in South
Africa.'

'*A son*,' repeated Lord Langdon with an extraordinary expression on his face.

'Yes. But perhaps you had forgotten him. I must admit that in view of the lapse of time since you last saw him, that would have been understandable. Perhaps you wished to forget him, as it suited him to forget you. He doesn't use your name. He passes under the name of Browning. It may be familiar to you.'

Lord Langdon's face first registered bewilderment; then, as the truth dawned, shock. Biggles gave him time to recover.

'Sit down,' said Lord Langdon in a curious voice.

'Thank you, my lord.'

'Are you telling me,' went on Lord Langdon, slowly, as if finding it difficult to articulate, 'that the man who worked here under the name of Browning was my *son*?'

'That is exactly what I am telling you.'

'Good gracious! Now I understand ...' Lord Langdon reached for the decanter and poured himself a stiff drink. He picked up a second glass. 'Will you join me?'

Biggles declined.

'So it was my own son who stole my rubies?' muttered Lord Langdon bitterly.

'He doesn't see it like that. He maintains that the rubies were not yours anyway; that they belong to his sister, the Lady Caroline. Is that correct?'

Lord Langdon ignored the question. 'Have you got the rubies?'

'No.'

'Have they been sold?'

'No.'

'Do you know where they are?'

'No. In the circumstances I preferred not to know. But I can tell you they're still in the family.'

'Does Lady Caroline know where they are?'

'I have reason to think so.'

'Have you spoken to her?'

'Not yet. I haven't had an opportunity. I hope to do so.'

'Then she knew who Browning really was!'

'Of course. He thought it advisable to tell her in view of your suspicions of their friendship, which you realize now was purely platonic.'

'I think,' went on Lord Langdon after a pause, 'you'd better tell me all you know.'

'That was really my purpose in coming here.'

Whereupon Biggles narrated what had happened in Africa. He did not spare Lord Langdon's feelings in the matter of why his son, after his fortuitous introduction into the household, had acted as he had. 'When Caroline said she didn't know where the jewels were, that was true at the time; but before I left England I knew she was in touch with Browning – or shall we now call him Richard? To be quite frank, my lord, if I may put it bluntly, the whole thing was a plan, a conspiracy if you like, on the part of Richard to prevent you from disposing of Caroline's inheritance and perhaps on your death leave her penniless. Richard didn't want the rubies. Nor does he now need money.'

Lord Langdon sat for a minute in silence. He still looked shaken. It was evident that he had not been prepared for anything like this. 'What are you going to do?' he asked at last.

'It isn't so much a matter of what I'm going to do, sir, as what you intend to do. It's up to you. Perhaps you'd like to think about it.'

'Is my son still in Africa?'

'I left him there. He won't run away. He gave me his assurance that should he move he'll leave a forwarding address with the police in Windhoek.'

'Is he likely to come here?'

'I very much doubt it, certainly not unless you invite him,

nd perhaps not then. After all, you can hardly expect him
o have any affection for you.'

Lord Langdon winced at the thrust. 'I suppose you're
ight,' he said sadly. 'I can see the blame for what has hap-
ened lies fairly on my shoulders; but there, we are all what
ve are, and that's the sort of man I am. What do you suggest
do?'

For the first time Biggles felt a twinge of sympathy for a
nan who was obviously distressed. 'Before you make up
our mind to do anything, I suggest I have a word with
Caroline. She should have a say in this matter. It may not
e too late for you to make amends. I'll prefer to see her
lone.'

'Why alone?'

'She may talk more freely to me if you were not present.
'm not proposing that I should act as a peacemaker, but it
eems a pity that in a small family like this a feud should be
llowed to persist. If this present attitude of animosity could
e dropped and you all come to some sort of understanding,
urely it would be better for everyone. Of course, that's
othing to do with me. For a start it might clear the air if I
old Caroline that I had seen Richard and was now in pos-
ession of all the facts. She may refuse to see me. I wouldn't
ress it.'

'Very well,' said Lord Langdon, a trifle wistfully. He rang
bell. To the footman who answered it he said: 'Give my
ompliments to Lady Caroline and say if she will see Inspec-
or Bigglesworth, he has news that should be of particular
nterest to her.'

The footman departed. They waited. He came back. 'The
ady Caroline will see Inspector Bigglesworth in her sitting-
oom.'

Biggles was taken to the room.

'I hope this isn't a trick to ask more questions,' greeted
Caroline coldly.

'On the contrary, I am now able to tell you something'
replied Biggles imperturbably. 'I thought you might like t
know I've had a long conversation with Richard.'

'Richard?' Caroline stared.

'Your brother.'

'Where?'

'In the Kalahari Desert.'

Caroline dropped all pretence of ignorance. 'How did yo
know where he was?'

'Let me give you a spot of advice,' went on Biggles, as
suming a confidential manner. 'When amateurs enter into
conspiracy, one of them usually slips up on a detail. Yo
did. But let us not go into that now. It is a good thing
found him, or it's unlikely you'd ever see him again. He wa
in pretty poor shape. He'd crashed and injured himself and
was being held more or less a prisoner by a queer charac
ter –'

'Connor?'

'Yes. So he told you about him?'

'Yes.'

'Well, Connor is dead. Richard is in hospital in Wind
hoek. He told me everything. Don't blame him for that. He
was in no condition to continue the deception. I have really
only come here to confirm a few details.'

'Have you told my father this?'

'As much as I thought he should know.'

'How did he take it?'

'On the whole very well. I think he's more subdued than
angry. Now do you mind if I ask a few questions?'

'What do you want to know?'

'First the rubies. You know where they are. I don't. Richard would have told me, but there were reasons why I didn't
want to know. Have you moved them?'

'Yes. Someone is taking care of them for me.'

'Your old nanny in the village, perhaps?'

Caroline's eyes opened wide. 'You're too clever,' she sighed.

'I'm a detective – remember?' Biggles smiled. 'Now tell me this, to satisfy me that the story Richard told me was true. Was Richard acting for you when he sold the ring to the jeweller in Bond Street?'

'Yes.'

'And he gave you the money?'

'Yes.'

'And you gave some of it back to him?'

'Yes.'

'Why?'

'To buy an aeroplane.'

'What did you intend to do with a plane?'

'Learn to fly. That was before I lent the plane to Richard to go to Africa. I thought when I was qualified I'd buy another plane and join Richard in Africa.'

Biggles shook his head sadly. 'Long-distance flights are not as easy as that, Caroline. But we needn't go into that. If you want to see Richard my advice is buy yourself a nice ticket and fly to Windhoek with one of the regular services. But for the moment the most important thing is to settle what is to be done about the rubies. It wouldn't be fair to leave it to an old woman to be responsible for them.'

'I'll put them in the bank.'

'Wouldn't it be better to discuss the whole thing amicably with your father and come to a clear understanding? I think you'll find his attitude very different from what it was.'

'Does my father know I have the rubies?'

'He must know you know where they are. He always knew that either you or Richard had them. He's not likely to take either of you to court. Knowing he has a son and heir has made him a different man, and I think you'll find him amenable to any suggestion you care to make, such as giving an undertaking that he won't sell any more of your jewels.

Talk it over with him. He might even invite Richard to come
here when he is well enough to travel – without masquer
ading as a footman. I gather they got on fairly well before
misunderstandings arose about your relationship. It should
be different now.'

Caroline thought for a moment. 'Very well,' she decided
'I'll take your advice.' She held out a hand. 'Thanks for
what you've done and the way you've done it. I suppose I've
been foolish, and rather rude to you. I'm sorry.'

Biggles smiled. 'That's all right. We all make mistakes
Let's leave it like that. By the way, if you do decide to take
up flying seriously come and see me. I may be able to give
you a few tips.' ·

'I'll remember it,' promised Caroline.

Biggles returned to the library. 'I've had a word with
Caroline,' he told Lord Langdon. 'She's going to discuss the
whole thing with you. Which means that everything is now
in your hands, and as there's nothing more for me to do, I'll
say good-bye, sir.'

That, as far as Biggles was concerned, was how the case of
the missing rubies ended. Some weeks later Richard called
on him. He was then staying at Ferndale Manor. He said he
was there at his father's invitation. The whole unhappy
business had been thrashed out. The family hatchet had
been buried and it had been agreed to let bygones be bygones. Which among reasonable and intelligent people is, of
course, the best way for family squabbles to be resolved.

These are other Knight Books

Five titles in the famous series by *Willard Price* about Hal and Roger and their amazing adventures in search of wild animals for the world's zoos.

UNDERWATER ADVENTURE
Helping a marine scientist explore the sea bed of the Pacific Ocean.

SOUTH SEA ADVENTURE
Sailing for the little-known islands of the west Pacific.

ELEPHANT ADVENTURE
Hunting for elephants on the Mountains of the Moon in Africa.

LION ADVENTURE
Battling with man-eating lions in Africa – and taking an unexpected trip in a balloon.

SAFARI ADVENTURE
Chasing big-game poachers on an African game reserve.

These are other Knight Books

THE EAGLES HAVE FLOWN

Henry Treece

Adventure, battles and intrigue in the Britain of 1500 years ago, with the army of Artos the Bear, the British chieftain who was the King Arthur of legend.

Illustrated by Christine Price

Ask your local bookseller, or at your public library, for details of other Knight Books, or write to the Editor-in-Chief, Knight Books, Arlen House, Salisbury Road, Leicester LE1 7QS